HER DRAWINGS

Joe Baldwin

For Sarah

The best sister

Summer was just underway, but the drought lingered on. The twentieth consecutive day without a drop of rain wasn't the day the two sisters should have ventured outside.

"Wait for me. It's hoooooot."

That whiny voice grated on Sally's nerves on a daily basis. And being out in the open field between the tall blades of grass instead of in their small house didn't make a difference.

"Well, you need to catch up, small legs," Sally said, teasing her little sister.

"I can't, Sally. It's hard for me. Please just stop," Rose said.

Sally figured her little sister could be relieved of abuse for at least the next couple of seconds. The grass was so tall that Sally could only see the pink bow their mom forced upon Rose's high ponytail bopping toward her.

"Okay, you're close enough now," Sally said and ran off.

Sally knew Rose was at her wits' end, and it was confirmed by her wailing cries. Sally paused and released an annoyed grunt. The last thing she wanted was to drag her little sister along on this journey, but if Mom came home early from her job and found Rose alone, Sally would be grounded until she was eighteen years old.

"Stop your crying. You're six and a half years old. That is the age you can't cry anymore. Didn't anybody tell you that?"

To Sally's surprise, she did stop. She was concerned as to why, but then she saw what her little sister saw. A single red rose. A perfectly textured and formed flower that any person would think up in their imagination when thinking of roses. The flower grew between the blades of grass. Sally broke her gaze for moment to collect her bearings. The edge of the forest, her destination, was a mere twenty feet away, but right now it felt like it would take an eternity to get there.

Rose plopped to the floor and looked up from a crisscross applesauce position, her eyes shimmering in the remainder of sunlight.

"It's a rose, like me."

"Yeah—" It was all Sally had for a response. A rose in the middle of a drought in the middle of a grassy field. An impossibility that Sally wasn't waiting around to figure out an answer to.

She was back to the age debate. Just like that. The snap of a finger. The odd flower forgotten.

"Nuh-uh. No one told me I can't cry anymore," Rose said.

"Well, it's the truth. Six and a half is when you become a big girl." Sally knelt and whispered into Rose's ear. "When I was six, Mom let me sit in the front seat of the car."

"Really?"

"Yup." What Sally failed to mention was they were in the driveway and the car wasn't moving. "So, if Mommy thought I was a big girl at six, then you definitely are."

That brought Rose back to her feet with a smile she rarely saw.

"But you didn't say where we are going," Rose said.

"I did tell you. I said we are going to my super-secret hideout. Just like in *Bridge to Terabithia*."

Rose was at a higher reading level than her entire class. Sally wasn't sure whose genes that talent came from, but it wasn't their mother. Rose's bedroom was filled with books from Pre-K up to a third-grade level. And *Bridge to Terabithia* was her favorite. She always yapped about it, and Sally was forced to watch the movie adaptation what must have been a hundred times.

"Really? Just like it?" The shimmer in her eyes returned, but the cause this time was utter excitement.

"Well, I can't promise traveling to a different world, but it is really cool."

"Where is it?"

"We're almost there."

Sally grabbed her sister's hand, mostly because she was tired of Rose slowing her down.

They darted through the large field, which started from their back yard and ended at the edge of the forest.

"Whoa."

Sally chuckled a bit. She had never heard Rose use that word or drop her tone to that inflection.

The uncertainty of the woods must've caused Rose to freeze. It didn't look like she feared the forest but the abandoned train track that preceded it.

"What's wrong?"

"I don't wanna get stuck there." She pointed to the track.

"You won't. Watch." Sally stood with her toes at the metal railing. She stepped one foot onto one of the wood sleepers and hopped, her red dress flowing freely in the breeze of her own doing, and landed safely on the other side. "See. It's easy."

"Sally, I can't do that. I'm too small."

"You can do it. It's not a far jump."

"No. You need to help me."

Sally rolled her eyes. She had been helping Rose with everything since the day she came into the world. Their mom forced Sally into a mother role of her own. Teaching Sally how to change diapers, feed, and lull the baby to sleep. Sally did more raising of Rose than their own mother did. And at the same age Rose was now. But apparently, she didn't do a good enough job.

"You need to do this on your own," Sally said. "What did I just say to you before? You are a big girl now and you need to learn how to do things by yourself. Now go. It's just a small jump. Go."

Rose adjusted the shoulder straps of the bookbag where she carried her reading books and her second-best pal, only to Sally, a stuffed elephant named Squirt. It was summer vacation, and Sally knew Rose wanted to sit in her room and read for the next three months.

Rose's eyebrows sloped inward, her mouth was smaller, and her nose scrunched. A face of determination.

She ran toward the track. Instead of placing a foot on one of the sleepers for an extra boost, she went for the entire leap all at once. From one metal rail to the other. The other was where she tripped and rolled. Sally stood inches away as her sister held her right arm and began her insistent howling.

"I think its broked. My arm. Ow, ow, ow, ow."

"Oh, get up. You're fine," Sally said, although she didn't know if Rose's arm was broken. "You landed in the soft grass."

"It really"—Rose paused to let in some sucking breaths—"hu-hu-hu-urts."

"Okay. Let's just go into the forest and we can—"

"No." Sally took a step back. She had never heard such aggression from her little sister. "We need to go home. Now."

Sally's gaze bored into the streaks of tears covering Rose's rosy cheeks. If Mom saw what Sally let happen to Rose, especially taking her to a place where Sally was forbidden, she wouldn't be grounded until she was eighteen; she would be willingly placed in the execution chair by her own mother.

"You are such a crybaby. My God. If you wanna go back to your mommy, then go. We're still basically in our back yard. I'm going to my secret place. I should of never brought you."

Sally marched into the forest where pines and spruces ate her up. A fork in the forest road split right and left. Left was the path to Sally's Manor, a treehouse she found when wandering while Rose and Mom were out. Rose was their mother's favorite. Sally and Mom used to go shopping and to restaurants together until Rose came along and ruined her life.

If she wanted to go home, then Rose was old enough to make those decisions. Sally was finished being her babysitter.

"Sally! Help!" The sheer fear of Rose's voice shook Sally and forced her around to look back at the edge of the forest.

Sally ran to the sound of Rose's ear-shattering shrieks. Yelps that no longer sounded like pain, but terror.

Back out by the track, there was nobody. Rose was nowhere in sight. Maybe she walked back toward home. But that scream.

Sally decided to do the walk home. Maybe Rose did decide to trek back home. But after the first few steps, she could hear a faint Rose again. It came from the edge of grass that spilled onto Asher Avenue.

The grass came up to almost her shoulders, so running at any great speed wasn't much of an option. She went along as fast as she could until she was spilled onto Asher. It was the street that intersected with Carbridge, where their home sat.

Perspiration poured down her face and was soaking her dress. The sweat came partially from the heat and partially from the thought of raging Momma waiting for her when Sally returned without her sister.

Asher held one side of houses, the other miles of grassy fields. It was mid-afternoon, and most cars were parked outside each respective home. She could knock on doors and ask if they saw a little girl walking—

Rose's screech again. Closer this time. But it seemed to be coming from back inside the tall grass. Was she playing a trick on her? Was this some kind of sick game Rose was playing on her older sister to get her back for being mean? She hoped not.

"Sally! Help!" The same call.

Sally disregarded the health of the grass. She bounded over the blades and stepped on the green foliage. She was getting to Rose this time.

When she made it back to the edge of the forest, she saw the back of a person. The long coat they wore was gray like they had rolled around in dust. Other features were blocked by the grown foliage.

"Hey," she said to grab the person's attention. The coat person turned slightly. Dangling from the crook of their arm was a strand of goldilocks blond hair. Rose.

The person continued inside the darkening woods, not at a quick pace, but Sally couldn't move. She could physically move, but she was held back by her own fear. Fear she hid from Rose, her mother, and kids at her school. Sally was a scaredy cat, and that fear struck her body so badly that moving wasn't an option.

That person had taken her little sister. Somebody she was supposed to protect for her entire life, and Sally couldn't do that because of her own ignorance.

All she could do was collapse to the ground, her top half in the edge of the tall grass and her bottom half in the hard soil facing the path of Rose and her abductor, who had to be beyond Sally's Manor by now.

As she lay there splitting her vision between the tall grass, a few steps away, she saw Rose's blue and purple stuffed elephant. It had fallen out of her bookbag. The only sign of her left behind.

As she stared at the stuffed thing, she began to do something she trained herself to hold only for her secret treehouse.

She cried

CHAPTER 2

Off Interstate ninety-five in Darien, Connecticut was the once renowned most visited rest area in the entire United States. When the residents flocked south on their daily ride to work in the big city, it was a place they could fuel their cars and their bodies as well as empty any remnants of the previous night's fluids and foods hanging around in their intestines.

After months of renovations adding new fast-food joints, new gas pumps, a convenience store, and arcade games the kids had no interest in playing, the number of daily customers plummeted. Nothing like a whole lot of money to drive people away from the establishment.

Although out of their control, an even deeper drop in patrons came on 2 PM on a Wednesday, February 15th. They were in the midst of a winter storm, which filled the highway with snow the plows found impossible keep up with.

Many travelers had pulled into the rest area to retreat from the trip they made the mistake of taking and wait out the remainder of the storm. Two men who appeared to be brothers sat at one of the tables meant for eating and were facing off in a game of Go Fish. Other patrons wandered, scrolling through their phones, staring out at the falling flakes, or reading newspapers. Maybe twenty people in total, including the staff. The McDonalds, Pizza Hut, Wetzel's Pretzels, Subway, and a generic restaurant that only sold mac 'n' cheese lined the outer walls, each with workers who looked to have been told they needed to pull a double shift.

All in the rest area had the same goal; get back home.

All except one.

This man stood out not because of his dirt-spattered face, or the odd pattern snaking through his skin. It was his lack of appropriate clothing. The plastic ski pants were suitable for the current weather conditions, but the ratted T-shirt made his arms redder than the door handle he opened to enter.

In his pockets he looked to have two water balloons incapable of breaking. With each step a jangle sound bounced from the beige tile floor to the open beam ceiling, giving away his private possession. Coins.

He shuffled past the many eating establishments, past the card-playing brothers who had stopped their game to view the odd man. When he reached the back section of the rest area where just outside the "cleanest bathrooms in the world," the sign proclaimed, were the arcade games.

A pinball machine clinked and clanked, calling for anybody to press its buttons. A game with a goal of stacking the quick moving animated blocks on top of one another was called "Play to win."

However, the only game the man showed interest in was the claw machine. He viewed the stuffed animals of various colors and varieties. He reached a dirty hand into his pocket and removed a silver quarter. The coin clinked to enter and clunked as it landed on the previous player's money. The machine woke, and the man used the joystick to set his target, a blue and purple elephant, then slammed on the down button. The claw descended, clipped the stuffed elephant, then returned to its home base empty.

The man would stay in that spot until the snow stopped falling and the blacktop returned to its original shade of

black. He needed that stuffed elephant, and with another
pocketful of quarters, he showed no signs of stopping
anytime soon.

CHAPTER 3

Sally Wilkinson sat where she sat each day at eight in the morning and had for the previous four years. In the corner of the ranch style home in an office with only a computer monitor, PC tower, keyboard, white table, and glass of hot herbal green tea.

Living in the real world wasn't as fun as they made it out to be growing up. When you were a child, you couldn't wait to grow up. When you were a teenager, you enjoyed your life a bit more. But, once you passed the remaining prime age of twenty-one, the fun ceased to exist. It was beyond schooling, beyond partying, and it was time to start your career. A career, a husband, a family: the American dream, as they said. But Sally wanted none of those things. Sally wanted to leave the real world as soon as she could. It was scary, and she found comfort in the fiction.

She used fiction as a way of coping with being tossed out of the one home she knew by her own mother at nine years old. It started with movies, then TV shows, and then she picked up a book. A hobby she never took interest in until after the incident. It was *Fifty Shades of Grey*, a book she snuck out of the local library. The important thing was that it was words on a page.

After being enthralled with the story, she craved more. She was a madwoman at Barnes and Noble each week for a new story to devour. Genres went out the window. She read romance, thriller, horror, Young Adult, even some middle grade. Then after years of filling her brain with all she could, Sally decided she could make one of her own. How hard could that be?

It turned out that it was incredibly difficult.

Her first story, which she self-published, crashed and burned. She thought it was a good story. Her best friend, Molly Mardito, thought it was "thrilling." But trusting friends to leave honest reviews was a giant mistake. And the small percentage of readers who found her book gave one- to two-star reviews. "Boring" and "confusing" were the top keywords used. Sally was ecstatic when she received a five star on Goodreads, until Molly called her to boast about the review she left, stemming from the free copy Sally had handed her. That destroyed her confidence.

Sally gave up writing for six months until she met a guy. This guy would change her life for the better. On their first date, Sally was reluctant to tell him she had any interest in trying to become a best-selling author, but he made her feel so warm and inviting that she spilled her embarrassment. They discussed the bad reviews, the hate in those reviews, and he said, "Fuck what everybody else thinks. If you enjoy doing it, then do it." It wasn't permission or validation from a man, a man who broke up with her months later, but it sure as heck motivated her. Motivated her enough to write every day, improve her craft, and get signed to a small publishing company.

Three novellas, two short story collections, and a door stop of a novel, which took her two years to complete, brought her to the same writing desk, staring at the cursor blinking back at her. A situation she found herself in many times. Only this time it felt as though her ideas, memories, and brain were locked away with the key nowhere to be found. She felt she couldn't shake whatever it was that had locked her up.

The buzz of her cell phone pulled her away from the screen, a grateful interruption. It was an area code she never wanted to think of again. A place her mother still resided, and a place Sally hadn't been in thirteen years.

With all the spam calls nowadays, it was par for the course to ignore unknown callers. And that was what she did. Minutes later she had typed a few words only to be interrupted by a tabletop vibration. A single one this time. The screen flashed, showing one voicemail. Curiosity always won in those situations. She pressed play.

"Miss Wilkinson, this is Sherrif Al Winters of the Redhill office. I'm sorry to bother you, but we have something in our possession that may belong to you. Please return my call at this number when you receive this message. You have a blessed day now."

The message ended, and Sally could only stare at the screen where the phone had shoddily transcribed what Sheriff Winters had said.

Why was she receiving the call when her mother lived in town? Maybe the intended recipient was her mother since the only acknowledgement was Miss Wilkinson. Though the town of Redhill was about proper greetings, so Missus Wilkinson would have been her mama.

Sally tapped the number in red indicating her previous missed calls and it rang. The scruffy-voiced Sherrif answered on the first ring. He was expecting her call back.

"Miss Wilkinson." A statement, not a question.

"Yes. This is Sally. You may mean my—"

"Missus Wilkinson is well known in these parts. As are you, Miss Wilkinson. You may not remember me, but I do you."

That was when her memories, like a machine that hadn't been running for years kicked into high gear. Her sister taken into the woods. Her mother crying and angry for years after. Sitting at the disgusting round kitchen table, being asked question after question and never providing an answer. Her escape into reading and writing hadn't been a desire to be rich and famous; it was a hobby that required no talking. While her mother threw chairs and harassed the sheriff's office to do "a goddammed thing" about her missing daughter, Sally didn't say a word for three years. Not to her mother, not to her schoolteacher, not even to herself. It caused great turmoil in that household, ultimately forcing Sally out to Connecticut to live with her Aunt Gertrude until she died. Sally was listed as the sole homeowner on the will and testament. A paid-off house on her own at eighteen years old. Her mother didn't speak with her again until the time she turned twenty.

"Miss—"

"Yes. I remember." She pulled herself from her reverie.

"Great. Let me just get down to it. The old place has been abandoned ever since…well, for a long while now. And I don't wanna have to be the one to tell you this if you still had any personal feelings for your former dwelling, but it's gone."

He took a long exhale as if that had been weighing on him for a time.

"Gone, how?"

"Arson. Somebody took Jose Cuervo with a rag hangin' out the mouth and torched the place good."

"Oh my God." Sally had lost all feelings for the old farmhouse she loved so much as a child but hated to hear about such an awful occurrence.

"That's right. What's left of the roof"—he said roof as *ruff*—"is charred to all hell. Forgive me, God. The walls flat on their backs, and Jesus, it's a lost cause."

"When did this happen?"

"Just this mornin'."

"Does my ma—"

"She knows. First person I called. She didn't seem too tore up about it. Given the circumstances and all."

There was a long silence between the two of them until Sherrif Winters broke through.

"But there was something salvaged in the rubble. It's…I don't know. Some kind of book. Looks like a kid's drawerings on the front. I didn't open it given the title."

"What's the title?"

"Sally's drawerings."

My drawings? But I never drew anything. Still don't draw anything.

"I never did that as a kid, but Rose—"

Her thoughts came to a stop. It was drawings from Rose *to* her.

"I did turn it around, and Rose's name was on the back side. I didn't wanna mention her name if—"

"Could you send it to me? I'll give you my address," Sally said, ignoring his niceties.

"I reckon I can get it to the postal service."

"Thank you. Thank you so much." The most excitement she heard from herself in ages.

"My pleasure, Miss Wilkinson. I also wanted to just take a second and say how sorry I am I was never able to catch the guy who took your—"

"Yeah. It feels wrong saying this, but that all feels like a distant memory now."

"Well, everybody's got their way of copin'. Another thing you should know about your mama—"

"Have a good day, Sheriff," Sally said and hung up.

She wasn't in the stable mental condition to hear about Momma.

When Sally ended the call, the flooding memories came, and they didn't stop. The piece of flesh she saw of the man running into the woods that day. The search parties of family members Sally never knew existed. The stuffed elephant. But mostly it was the hope that returned. The hope that Rose was still out there somewhere. The hope that she would finally find her sister again.

CHAPTER 4

The anticipation of something from her sister on its way only worsened her writing procrastination. She had only just hung up the phone and she was wanting to go out and start the search again. Gather the neighbors, call her short list of friends, and get the local police involved. But all that would be for naught. Rose was surely dead in a ditch along the side of some abandoned highway. And most importantly, Sally couldn't do that to her mother.

After the ten years of the cold shoulder from her own mom, Sally received that first phone call from her mother. There was no mention of Rose, no mention of the investigation, nothing. It was as though she woke up on that day and her memory bank dumped its funds into the trash. A daughter named Rose never exited her mouth then or any other time they spoke on the phone. Sally would bring up Rose, but Momma would pause for a scary number of minutes and move on about her own life.

It caused a twinge deep in Sally's stomach each time she saw "Mom" on her caller ID. It would be an hour of her complaining about the same people she had worked with at the same job for the past five years, and then she hung up and waited another week to make the same call about the same topics.

"Andy keeps staring at my ass, and if he doesn't stop, I'm calling HR."

"Jessica thinks she's so pretty with her big boobs and five-star husband. Give me a trash to vomit into."

New week, new story, same boring people.

The taking of Rose hadn't left Sally's mind; how could it? It tortured her mind each waking morning. She watched a man stomp away while she sat on the ground like a coward and looked on as it happened. It was like a TV show where she was helpless against the bad guy in that episode. And that was what it became in her mind. A long-lost episode in her life.

When Sally was living in the Redhill home, every day was a struggle. Every day she would hole herself in her room and refuse a word with anybody. Even when she was forced at the kitchen table across from the chubby deputy asking her what happened, she wouldn't budge.

"What happened there, Sally? You're not in any kind of trouble; we just wanna help find your little sister. You do want that, don't you?"

Sally had nodded her head, but she wasn't listening to what he was saying. She focused on anything other than what was happening in the present. The tick of the round clock above the door crest leading to the dining room, the sobs of her mother from the living room, the jowls jumbling around the neck of the deputy.

"Great. He took her off into the woods, then what happened?"

Sally shrugged. Not because she was being a brat the way some kids did at her age, but because she honestly didn't know. After the last of the silhouette disappeared between the chipped trunks, Sally lay back in the tall grass, and like she was inside a washing machine, the blue sky twisted and pulled, triggering a dizzying lightheadedness. The embarrassing tears rolled down her cheeks. She lay that way until her mother's angry face appeared above her. Her short brown hair dangled like a halo hovering over her face. The distorted lips and crow's feet brow split was the most enraged she had ever seen her mother. Even after she broke the flower vase in the living room after the deputies called off the search.

"Where is Rose?" Her mother's voice had sounded like Sally was underwater. As if her voice was calling from a great distance. Sally had no memory of how she returned to the home, but there she sat at the stripped wood of the small round kitchen table, speaking with Deputy Jowls. Squirt was tossed on the kitchen counter upside down. Sally played a useless round of a staring contest while she drowned out the realness suffocating her.

"And there ain't no things that stood out like tattoos or anything like that he had?"

One aspect of the entire three years she remained silent, Sally was proud of one proven fact. She never lied to anyone. Not even her head nods and shakes told a fib. Sally remained still during that question because the man did have a special marking. Just under the Barbie blonde strand of Rose's hair along the outer forearm, the man had a white, fleshy marking. It looked to Sally like she could see through his skin to his bones.

And there was one more thing from that day she left out of any investigations. One thing she regretted not bringing up to this day. She saw a glimpse of the man's face.

Karen White had been a Darien resident for all her fifty years. Born in Stamford Hospital and brought back to her father's cozy Darien Cape Cod, she was an only child and got anything she asked for. Her father couldn't say no, and now anybody who said no to her was an instant enemy.

The clerk at the Darien I-95 rest area was her newest rival. Karen wanted the white cheddar popcorn, it was her favorite, but they were out of stock.

"And when does it go back into stock?" she demanded.

"We typically get deliveries on Tuesdays, but—"

"Today is Wednesday. How does a product sell out in one day?"

The bored associate shrugged his scrawny shoulders. His minimum wage bi-weekly check didn't motivate him enough to explain that one man had bought all twenty bags off the shelf.

"I would ask to speak with your manager, but I'm sure they are as incompetent as you are."

Karen clutched her purse close to her as she stormed back into the open restaurant area.

On the way back to her BMW, she spotted the arcade tucked in the rear of the rest area. She knew it was there. She did her snack and sundry shopping there since the gas stations by her home didn't fulfill her request for her favorite type of popcorn.

She entered the area where a small child was mashing his hands against the sides of the pinball machine. The clinking and whapping of the metal ball against the plastic whackers was making her migraine grow increasingly worse.

Where was that child's parents anyhow?

Beyond the child was the claw machine. Stuffed elephants, stuffed bears, stuffed octopi all up for grabs encased in that glass box.

She stopped, and the bottom of her mink coat whisked the back of her ankles.

The man operating the machine was the most grotesque individual she had ever laid her eyes upon. He couldn't be described as pale. He was a painter's white. And his skin appeared flaky. The winter storm on the outside had ended, but this monster had a snow cloud hovering over him. And his arm. A strange marking. Almost like a snake had been branded to his bicep. But it was iridescent.

All that had dissipated once she saw what had been littered all around him. Empty bags of white cheddar popcorn. Must've been twenty bags that encircled him. Crushed, crumpled, unfinished aluminum polypropylene angered her to no end.

She had wanted to try her hand at getting her newborn granddaughter a new friend she could squeeze to her heart's content, but Karen was the one who wanted to squeeze that man-thing's head until it popped.

"Hey," she said.

No acknowledgment. He continued to enter coins through the slot and begin a new game. He wasn't just enthralled; he had removed himself from what the others called the real world. He only existed to retrieve that stuffed elephant from the claw game.

"Excuse me. I am speaking to you." As the words left her mouth, the elephant fell from the grasp of the claw and back into stuffed animal purgatory.

He turned, his face a mask of anger that caused Karen to take a couple steps back in her three-inch-heeled thigh high boots. His face looked to have been sewn that way. Eyebrows indented. Red spotted mouth turned downward. Wrinkles rippled like the ocean waves.

Karen stepped back a few more steps when he wouldn't stop his staring. It was like a creepy painting by an artist showing off their highest quality work.

He entered another coin, moved the claw, pressed the drop button all while affixing his gaze on her.

She scuttled around the corner, so she was out of view of him. She rustled through her Prada bag and removed her cell phone. She dialed 911.

Forty-five minutes later, a state trooper sauntered into the rest area. Karen frantically waved her arms as if he didn't know who placed the call. Being a Darien resident outside of the cozy town limits, she stood out against the travelers going to and from their destinations.

"What's goin' on?" the trooper asked. His gray uniform and blue tie were neatly pressed and his pins shining against the incredible lighting. A campaign hat clutched to his chest.

"That man back there threatened me," she said.

"Threatened you how?"

"He—I don't know. The way he was looking at me. It looked like he wanted to hurt me."

"But he didn't say anything to you?"

"No. Why don't you do your job and go talk to him."

"I'm just trying to gather as much information as I can," the trooper said and rounded the corner into the arcade room.

"Excuse me, sir. Can you step away from the game for a minute?"

The man continued to operate the joystick, ignoring the officer's request.

As another coin dropped inside, the trooper said, "Sir, I am not asking you."

The tonality of the trooper's voice and of the rest area changed within seconds.

The man turned, his crazy black eyes like a vise grip on the stumpy, plump trooper. The thing opened its mouth, and stringy liquid clung to the gums of missing teeth as he spoke.

"AHHHHGHTERTHINGH!"

The nonsensical wording and a movement in the trooper's direction forced him to draw his service weapon. The size of the thing that didn't appear quite human was apparent when it stood three feet over the law enforcement officer.

An arm as thick as a tree branch struck the trooper, and he slid across the white polished floor like he was on a zipline and slammed his back into the pinball machine. He was dazed but remained conscious. The blow caused his weapon to skitter across the linoleum between the thing and Karen, who was watching like it was a spectator sport.

The thing disregarded the gun and started for Karen. The tree branch arm came again, but before it made contact with her shocked, stoned face, a report rang out, deafening anyone within the building. Although most patrons had retreated to the outside.

A hole formed in the center mass of the thing. A blue liquid leaked from its body, and it returned to its normal human size before collapsing to the ground.

It had transformed down to a normal human man.

Karen sat up on her arm to locate the source of the impact that drug her to the ground. The clerk she berated earlier had taken her out of harm's way of the flying bullet and the thing. She smiled at the kid and then turned toward the thing.

The monster was dead.

CHAPTER 6

Growing up, Sally had a fascination with the mailbox. Their baby blue box—painted shoddily by Rose—sat at the end of their twenty-foot-long dirt driveway. Sally sat reverse on the couch, watching and waiting for the oddly shaped mail truck to drop the letters inside. Then she would race outside before Mr. Stacy, the local mailman, had time to close the door to his truck. He would wave as Sally retrieved the mail and ran back into the house. There was rarely anything for her, except when she and Rose got letters from their grandfather in Michigan. Sally loved the handwritten letters that she got from G'pa Bob. Grandpa Bob had the worst handwriting, so Mom would have to translate.

After the incident, the letters stopped. Sally never ran to get the mail. Neither did Mom. It piled up enough for Mr. Stacy to knock on the door and hand deliver it to Momma.

"Terribly sorry for your loss," Sally remembered Mr. Stacy saying to Momma.

"Loss? My baby's not dead. She's missin'. Are you implyin' somethin', Mr. Stacy?" Momma said.

"No. Of course not. Terribly sorry."

That was the last Sally saw of Mr. Stacy. A different, meaner-looking man dropped off the mail for the rest of the time she lived at home.

The sliding door and slam of a mail truck snapped her from her musing and back to Connecticut. The mailbox at the end of the much shorter driveway was the standard operating model. A solid white cave that had been filled for the day.

In her bare feet, like she did at the age of eight, she ran to the mailbox and swung it open.

"Waitin' on something?" the mail carrier, a young woman with blonde curls, said.

"Oh yes," Sally said, emptying the contents.

An *Ulta Beauty* magazine she was forced to acquire when she went in for one tube of mascara that she wore on one date. Two envelopes with no markings other than: URGENT: ONLY THE INTENDED PARTY CAN OPEN. Those were going straight into the trash. And one final package. A manila envelope with the return address of Redhill. This was it.

She sprinted back inside, hopping when her heel caught on a pebble. It was always the smallest rocks that hurt the most.

She tore the perforated edge from one side, reached inside, and pulled out a stack of about ten papers. They were bound together by a row of staples. On the front in poor child's handwriting was SALLY'S DRAWINGS by ROSE WILKINSON. Underneath the title was a drawing of two people in crayon. On the right, Sally assumed, was supposed to be her. A triangle body, depicting the dresses Sally used to wear, an oval head with brown hair fanned out on each side, two dot eyes, a smiling mouth, and two stick legs. The shading Rose tried her hand at was a frantic tornado of art terribly outside the border lines.

Drawn Sally had stick hands with a shorter version of the same drawing. But Rose's depiction of herself was a red dress with a red bow in her blonde hair. The golden yellow crayon she used was much duller than her real beautiful locks.

A copse of green trees filled the background of the two girls.

Sally was struck with a choked-up sob of emotions looking at the front cover. The outfits were exactly what they were wearing on the day Rose went missing. The same colors anyhow. That was impossible. Sally didn't have a large rotation of clothing, but there was no way she could have known the exact color of both their outfits.

A pain fell to her lower abdomen. She didn't want to open it. She was struck by a pang of fear of what could be inside. Why was she worried? It was a child's drawings; what was the worst that could possibly happen?

That, Sally Wilkinson, was about to find out.

CHAPTER 7

Rose loved to learn new things. She had been a sponge for information ever since she was three years old. At three, she was talking in complete sentences and using phrases her momma had used once before.

"You don't know shit from Shinola," her momma would say.

The next day Rose bopped over to her momma, looked her dead in the eye, and said, "Shit Shinola."

Momma had laughed so hard that had she been drinking milk, it would have jetted from all her openings.

The teachers at Redhill Elementary would call Momma each semester to rave about how much of a brilliant child she had. Rose was the first child in the school's history to perform a perfect year. A perfect score on every test she was given. No matter if it were math, science, or social studies. The math teacher had even slipped in a third-grade level question on one of Rose's tests and she nailed it.

The one negative that would come up in each report card's notes was her attention. Rose's head was constantly looking down while she scraped a pencil against a sheet of paper. She would bring her crayons to class and color while she was supposed to be paying attention to the lesson. After a while the teachers would let her draw since it failed to affect her grades.

Then she would get home, select a book from the shelf in her room, and read until it was time for bed. Momma had gifted her the books she read when she was Rose's age.

Rose told Momma she was bored with those books and needed something tougher. Momma was floored by the admission. Momma couldn't get properly through those books until at least the fifth grade. Though Momma would be the first to tell them that she didn't have the best education growing up.

Momma began giving Rose third-grade level reading and continued from there. Rose blew through all of them, and eventually the books stopped coming. Rose was devasted. The thing she loved the most was forced to a screeching halt. Re-reading wasn't in her DNA, so she took matters into her own hands.

One day Rose and Sally were home alone, which was typical when the school bus would drop them off and Momma wouldn't be home for another hour. Sally wasn't old enough to babysit her baby sister, but Momma figured they would be fine.

"Rose. Rosey," Sally had called in a singsong tone.

"What? I'm right here."

Sally rounded the hall into the living room where Rose pretended to read a book she had finished two days prior.

"Ashlee is stopping over, so I will be outside," Sally said.

"Momma said no friends," Rose said.

"She's not coming inside. We are gonna talk on the porch."

"Still no friends."

"You're not in charge anyhow. I am. And you know what that means?"

Rose didn't like when Sally was condescending toward her. But that was just how she spoke.

"I'm still tellin' Momma," Rose said, and Sally stormed off out the front door to wait for her friend.

Rose really wanted Sally to leave because she had a plan.

Rose sauntered to the basement door. The Yale lock was
a bit out of reach, but Rose could go up on her tippy toes and
use the key from the drawer to unlock the metal device. She
had tried a week prior, but Momma had come home early,
and she had to smack it locked again.

She pulled and the lock came undone. She smacked the
rusted lock, and it lifted from the doorframe. The door to the
basement creaked open. She stuck the lock and key in her
overalls' breast pocket. When she peered down the steps, all
she could see was darkness. There should have been a light
switch, but Rose would do the zombie walk to guide her
way down.

Hands out in front and ten steps later, she had reached the
bottom. The remaining sunlight through the basement
window pointed her in the direction of the downstairs
switch. She flipped it up, and fluorescent beams flickered to
life.

The cement floor was cold on her stockinged feet. She
searched around the damp, dark place. She had heard
Momma discuss the adult books her momma had read before
she died. Rose needed those books.

In one corner sat a white, grimed chest freezer. A chain
looped around its body with a lock securing it tight. Rose
had read stories about death and what happened to that
person afterward. They were kept in a place in the hospital
that was like a large freezer and stored bodies instead of
food. Rose ignored the freezer and walked to the opposite
side when she located what she came looking for.

Through the window she could hear laughter. Ashlee had
a laugh like no other, a laugh that cured anyone's sadness.
Rose thought the neighbors on Willow Road could hear her

glee. And that was miles away. Rose wished they would
lower their chatter so she could hear if Momma was coming
home. Not many cars traveled up the street, so any revving
engine and Rose would need to bolt upstairs.

If Momma found her in the basement, she would be
punished for the rest of her life. But if Sally was caught with
a friend over the house, she would only get a talking to.
Rose wanted to use her advantages of being the younger
sibling, but the basement was forbidden for all.

"You could get hurt down there," Momma always said.

As she opened the first cardboard box, the stench of
uncared for paper hit her. A mix of grass and vanilla. It
drifted through her nose and into her mind, and she was no
longer worried about punishment. She was in her element.
What must've been one hundred books were stacked inside.

Stephen King, Margaret Atwood, Cormac McCarthy,
Judy Blume, and so many more. She was picking them out
one by one and placing ones that sounded interesting in a
pile. Before she knew it, the stack was taller than she was.

After much deliberation, she decided on one. *Firestarter*.
About a girl who could set things on fire with her mind. A
well of excitement burst through her as she hugged the dusty
book to her chest. That well turned to fright when a bang
frightened her. The book fell out of her hands and thudded
to the ground. She thought Momma had come home, but the
conversation between Sally and Ashlee outside had
continued. The noise was close. The noise was across the
basement.

Again. One sudden thump, then silence.

Rose turned and stared at the chest freezer. She watched
it for what must've been a few minutes. Then, she not only

heard the sound this time but saw it. The lid of the freezer lifted, but the chain held it in place. She approached the freezer, her eye level even with the opening. When it lifted, she saw a pair of eyes staring at her for a split second. They weren't human eyes. The eyes of a creature. Its pupils were vertical slits and its skin looked green and slimy. She wasn't scared. She was enthralled.

The slam of the front door and a car door meant Sally was back inside, and Momma was close behind. Rose left the stack of books and the cover of her next read, eyeballs between a tent of flame, staring up at the basement's leaking insulation.

"What are you doing? Momma's going to kill you," Sally said, waiting for her sister at the top of the stairs.

Rose ignored her. Her only mission was getting the lock back on so Momma would never find out she was down there.

She jumped, frantic to get the lock back into its proper function. But she wasn't getting the lift she had when she first went to explore the depths of the house.

"Help," Rose said, out of breath.

The door was opening, and fear hit her for the first time. The real monster was entering the front door.

Sally reached above Rose and connected the device into the locking position. Then her big sister pulled her into the kitchen where she went into the fridge and handed Rose a drink.

Her momma never suspected a thing.

But mommas always had a way of knowing things.

This time Rose knew a secret Momma was keeping in the basement that Rose was going to uncover one way or another.

CHAPTER 8

Sally needed to look at her hands one more time to confirm what she was seeing was real. A scribbled tan color scraped over the black outline fingers that made up her hands. Her arms were uneven lines leading to nonexistent shoulders. Her outfit, a red dress, was difficult to move in as it moved mechanically with each step she took. The world around her filled with paper grass blades, a green sky above, and a yellow sun in the upper left-hand corner. The sun, rays that were lines placed around the circle, stayed still as she maneuvered her way deeper into the tall grass.

Where was she?

That was a difficult question. Not to answer, but to comprehend. She knew where she was. She just didn't want to believe it. She was inside the drawing on the first page of the book she had received from Sheriff Winter in the mail.

This was an impossibility. The last thing she remembered doing was separating the pages, which felt as normal as paper could feel, and like a sleep that snuck up on an exhausted individual, she was there. A small glance was the best look she got of the artwork. But maybe that was all it was. A dream. A fabrication of life in a world with no consequences. Somehow it felt real. Somehow, she knew it was real.

Sally had taught Rose how to draw when she saw her little sister grasping a crayon in a fist and scribbling nonsense lines. Sally wasn't the best teacher since she wasn't even close to being an artist of any kind, but it was quality time with her younger sister she sorely missed when she was gone. A house was the first drawing Rose created.

"Here," Sally had said, taking a paper from the printer and the crayon. "First you start with a square. It can be as big or as small as you want. Then, you draw a triangle on top. A rectangle for the door. Smaller squares for windows and crosses to make smaller square windows called panes."

"Pain?" Rose had asked.

"No. Not that kind of pain." Rose had given her a blank stare that was adorable and scary. As if she had just opened her eyes to a whole world of possibilities. And that was what happened. Rose began with the house, then added trees, then added people, then her mind opened, and it spilled onto her canvas. Sally imagined a time when she was older and how she would own a studio where she would express her feelings through her art. If only. Her writing was her art, but her memory bank was stretched thin.

The picture Sally was venturing through glided with each movement. As she crested a looping green knoll, the very house Sally had taught her to draw was there in all its lopsided glory. It was shaded brown and the size of a small shed. As she approached, the ugly green sky looked to be traveling with her. A never-ending work created by a devoted artist. The shed grew bigger with each paper step.

When she reached the rectangle door, a poorly colored circle was serving as the doorknob. Sally gripped it, and it felt rough in her hands. It felt like sandpaper. She turned it, and miraculously the door creaked open. Like pushing cardboard against a dirt yard, a real dirt yard.

Inside the shed was a crudely drawn depiction of their old home's basement. Sally had been down there three times in her lifetime. The first time was because she was curious. Out of the blue, her momma was adamant about Rose and her staying out of there, but that made Sally want to go down more. Momma locked it up, but she wasn't good at hiding the key.

The gray cylinder hot water heater sat on her immediate right once she reached the bottom. Boxes marked "books" sat in the far-right corner behind a stone pillar. In the left corner was a red, chipped tetanus-inducing boiler. On the left was one white ice chest freezer. When Sally first saw the chains wrapped around multiple times, it freaked her out so much she ran back upstairs, never to return.

As she reached the top landing, she swore she heard a thump come from inside that freezer. She didn't want to ask any questions because she was too freaked about any possible answers.

The second time she visited the dungeon was to retrieve a ball that had snuck down there. Sally and Rose were kicking a soccer ball their momma had gifted Sally for her seventh birthday. Rose kicked it so hard it lifted the basement window and the ball dropped inside. Sally had removed the lock, ran down, grabbed the ball, shut the window, and ran back upstairs. In the corner of her eye, the freezer chest lid lifted and fell back down. She had her horse blinders on for that trip, but the ever so slight movement caused her skin to crawl until she was back outside. She hated being down there.

The final time was the day Rose was taken. Over the weeks since Momma had locked them out of the basement, Sally knew Rose was visiting. Rose would wait for the first opportunity of alone time and slip inside. The closest she got to being caught was the time Momma came home as she was attempting to lock up. Sally had a moment of guilt when she saw Rose struggling and wanted with every fiber in her being to let her get caught. But compassion swelled her, and she reached up to lock it for her. The way Rose peered up at her made Sally's heart sing. Rose was a pain in her side, as most younger sisters were, but they were in the same life situation, and two versus one ruled.

After the police were long gone and Momma had fallen asleep—each snore that left Momma's throat was another reason Sally felt that Momma didn't care much for Rose, Sally slipped out of her room. The time on the clock said 2:44 AM.

She found the key and slipped into the cold, dank, dreary hole in the earth. If Rose wasn't afraid, then neither was Sally. She reached cold cement floor on her bare feet. She went straight to the freezer and halted when she found the chain snaked on the ground and the lid wide open. It was empty. Whatever was in there had escaped. Or somebody had helped it escape.

Staring at the paper freezer drawn with the lid open, Sally was beginning to think the worst.

For Rose.

And for herself.

CHAPTER 9

It wasn't a dream.

Like a cocoon unraveling and revealing the beautiful butterfly beneath the ugly surface of what was once a caterpillar, Sally unspooled onto her living room floor. She landed at the rear of the green couch she referred to as her *Shrek* couch. And just like a butterfly, the caterpillar's thoughts of depression and feelings of unwantedness were released, just as Sally's were. She was cooped up inside, afraid to venture back out into the world. Afraid she would hurt somebody else with her lack of attentiveness. Writing was her safe haven because she could escape into the fictional places inside her own head for a little while.

She never considered physically traveling into the stories she wrote. That was an impossibility. An impossibility that her writer mind couldn't even fathom.

"What just happened?" she asked her empty home.

The colored book sat feet away from her. She was afraid to move it or even touch it. She didn't want to be sucked back inside. But it was only when she opened it that she was sucked into that place imagined by her missing younger sister.

Sally stood and went into the kitchen. She retrieved cooking tongs and carefully lifted the book, holding it gingerly. She carried it to her office where she wrote and retrieved a large envelope from her drawer. The envelopes she would use to submit her completed manuscripts to agents and publishers. It was the first time it was filled with another's work, and she was grateful for it to be her little sister's.

When she was assured of her safety, she threw it on the side table and booted up her computer. Her proceeding actions were some that churned her stomach to simply think about. She purchased a plane ticket to Redhill. She packed her clothes, the envelope, and a special treat into a rolling suitcase. She emptied her drawers. She wasn't sure if she would chicken out at the door or stay in Redhill for good. She knew the former wasn't a possibility. Sally knew whom she needed to talk to. It would be tough, but if the book was a sign that led her closer to where her sister might be, she couldn't risk living the rest of her days with the guilt.

Momma, I'm coming home.

***

An hour-and-a-half flight was a pointless air affair. By the time the plane was revved up, taxied, and in the air, it was time to descend. There was no time for a full-length film, and Sally only had two bites of her airplane cookie. The adventure was less about the time limit and more about her stomach flipping and flopping.

One year ago, she went on a national book tour for her novel with stops sporadically across the United States. Attendance was low, but she was proud to be such a young author to be able to make stops and have strangers commend her work. During the trip, she was on a plane every day for two weeks straight for a minimum of three hours. She never got used to that feeling of being thirty thousand feet above the earth, but modern-day planes had too many distractions to care.

Momma lived in the countryside. It was a one-mile trip from the farmhouse where Sally grew up. Sally would visit Rose's bedroom when unsavory activities were happening behind the walls, and they would talk about their life in Redhill. Sally would complain about the annoying kids at school and the lack of activities within the town. Rose never complained, but she told Sally one time that she saw a video of California and said she wanted to live there. It turned out to be a resort in Barbados, but the commercial she saw mentioned flights from California. That caused a chuckle in Sally. Rose was so innocent, and as the plane taxied in, Sally began to tear up. She was going to find her sister if it was the last thing she ever did.

Sally rented a car since Momma's home was a twenty-five-mile trip from the airport. The city buildings with their head in the clouds soon gave way to homes the middle class would favor. But the country was Momma land. No more paved roads. No more grocery stores. No more businesses. Just rough-looking homes, dead grass, and the old standpipe.

The west side of Redhill looked as it did when it was founded in 1878. The homes weren't inaccessible nor was the convenience store in the middle of town, but it was a dump.

As the politicians took and subsequently exited office, no matter their affiliation, Redhill was turning to big business and less farmland of old. Some residents fought back. They marched in circles around the brand-new Redhill town hall when it was the west side's turn for destruction and rebuilding. They fought strong until the officials backed down and left the small portion to live on as they wished. It was a laughable situation.

She was traveling down the Palasky Turnpike, the main highway in Redhill, then all of a sudden dropped from paved blacktop to a dirt rocky path.

The rental car place wouldn't be happy with the caked-on dirt the sedan's body had already accumulated. Sally feared she would need to pay a fee when she returned it, but that was the least of her worries.

Redhill West, as the locals called it, was its own little town in and of itself. It reminded Sally of the campgrounds she stayed at during some of the stops on her book tour. It was a change of pace from the same boring hotel rooms. The campgrounds had built-in homes for rent, and those were times Sally wished she could get back.

Momma's current living situation came up first. A boring bungalow with a single window and a small wood door not yet painted. A perfect quaint place for somebody like Momma who lived alone and loved to be alone. Her yard was a mess of dead grass, and it worried Sally to see her mailbox door swinging open, filled with envelopes and magazines. Momma was never one for venturing out to the mailbox, so Sally was convinced she picked it up on a weekly basis or when one of her far-off neighbors brought it to her stoop.

Sally drove on another mile until she saw it. The farmhouse she had many good and bad memories inside and out.

The neighborhood of old she knew so well had taken a turn for poverty and hollowness. The town had failed to fund Redhill West since they gave in to the citizens' demands. The grass where Rose would chase her when they played a game of tag was pale brush. It looked like a forest fire waiting to happen or one that already did. The front stoop remained intact among the rubble of destruction where she and her best friend Ashlee would conversate about their classmates and whom they would kiss. It was like she had stepped into a time machine. A past that had been told through the mind of a dystopian author.

The surrounding homes she remembered on Asher Avenue didn't survive the political outrage. The homes of the families that found the deteriorating conditions of Redhill West debilitating abandoned house and were given a hefty check toward a new one. The empty dwellings were destroyed and removed. Momma's old farmhouse, three other ranches on Carbridge, spattering houses throughout the five-mile stretch of leftover western land, and a rundown convenience store were all that remained. Sally had a vision of seeing her old treehouse now that most of the land was flat. Her dreams were crushed when green had been removed from this section of town's color palette.

She parked along the edge of the lifeless lawn of the wrecked farmhouse and exited. When she reached the yellow caution tape surrounding the exterior, she ducked underneath without hesitation. As far as she was concerned, this was still her home. No matter how little structure remained. She peered out at the piles of charred rubble. Her focus was the basement. Without a construction vehicle to remove the debris, there was no way she was viewing Rose's old hangout. Sally wasn't giving up; she was simply putting it on hold.

The conclusion of winter had just arrived, but the evening chill lingered. It forced Sally to hurry back to the car and drive the mile back to Momma's new digs. She had a driveway Sally felt comfortable enough parking in. She flung a drawstring backpack on herself, marched back out to the road, and with a twinge of nostalgia and anguish, retrieved the mail and swaddled it like a baby in her arms.

When she reached the porch, she dropped it on the floor. Some of the envelopes fell into the dead bed of dried-up bushes and flowers.

While maneuvering the streets was as easy as it was in childhood, she hadn't realized the dark that encompassed her. It was evening, but full dark was close behind. The impossibilities of viewing anything through momma's single window told Sally that was how momma lived her life as well. In the shadows.

Sally knocked on the door. Momma didn't like surprises. She never did. As she heard someone approaching, Sally had so many questions firing off inside her brain.

Would she recognize me?

Would she remember me?

Would she want to speak with me?

The door creaked open. A single eyeball peeked through the open slot. A green color with a pupil the width of a chopstick.

A tired, wretched voice spoke from the darkness of the home.

"I knew you'd come back."

CHAPTER 10

From the first time Rose bounded down the basement steps, she never went a day without going down there. She used to read books on her bed. Then she graduated to the dirty living room couch. Then when all the kids' books were in her mind's eye, a small circle rug she found in the basement became her newest and most favorite spot for the adult literature.

Firestarter by Stephen King opened her mind to innumerable possibilities. She never knew what a full-length novel could be until she read that story. The grotesque actions by many of the characters, the life little Charlie lived she found was quite similar to hers. Charlie was stubborn, and Rose felt she was the same, particularly to her sister. Charlie was smart, and Rose, reading a grown-up novel and understanding it, felt the same way. And Charlie was strong. Though Rose didn't have pyrokinetic powers, she felt she didn't need anything supernatural to prove she could fight anybody or anything and win.

A thump.

Momma was getting up from bed. During Rose's reading times, typically between three and five in the morning, Momma had gotten up several times to use the toilet. She had heard the flush and Momma trudging back to bed. This time instead of crossing over Rose, crisscross on the nasty rug, book splayed open across her lap, Momma was stepping away from her. Toward the kitchen. Momma loved her midnight snacks, but this was not one of those times.

The latch on the door banged against the wood of the trim. Momma never passed by the door on her bathroom trips, so Rose figured the missing lock wouldn't be noticeable for her few reading hours. Rose was facing the door when the squeal of the handle turning caused her to bolt behind the boxes of books, *Firestarter* still in hand.

Rose peeked between two stacks of books and cardboard boxes as Momma limped her way to her level. Momma had bad knees, but that never stopped her from being the most terrifying force in Rose's life.

"I know you're down here," Momma said.

Rose clamped her palm over her mouth to avoid making a sound. The chest freezer that periodically went bump in the night was Momma's first stop. Momma reached into her bosom and revealed a necklace with a skeleton key dangling at the end of the rope. Rose had searched high and low for the key to unwrap the chest freezer but could never locate it.

Momma stuck the key into the rusted lock. "Last chance to reveal yourself. You seem so interested, so how's about I show you instead."

The novel Rose had stuck between her legs dropped with a thud.

Momma turned her gaze. It looked like she was staring at Rose as she turned and popped the lock open but made no indication.

The chain came undone within seconds, and Momma opened the top. From what Rose could see, it appeared empty. All the times she heard shuffling and what sounded like something running laps inside, it couldn't have been nothing all along?

Then Momma did something strange. She stuck her arm inside. It was like she was reaching for a frozen dinner she was going to prepare for the kids. Instead, she was pulling an arm from inside. It wasn't a human appendage that rose from the depths.

As the thing's head crested the top of the freezer, Rose knew she wasn't dealing with a he or her, but a monster.

The thing's brown pupils morphed into a slimy green color. The circular irises shrank to vertical slits. Every pore grew bumps and scales. Its epidermis turned a pastel yellow as though it had a kidney issue. The muscles on its arms and legs expanded and contracted tendrils of meaty flesh. The thing's fingers developed into white claws. Its clothes tore at the seams and confettied to the hard, cool ground.

Whatever thing was in the freezer had reacted to a gentle touch from Momma. It had fully awakened.

The thing squealed through its contracted mouth in an ear-piercing screech. Then it moved across the floor quicker than Rose had expected. Rose shot for the stairs. Its claw nails clicked in hot pursuit.

As Rose reached the top step to freedom, a warm thing clamped her ankle and drug her down. She stopped herself from tumbling to the bottom. She scraped her palm and panicked that she would contract tetanus from the rotting wood and the reddened nails not entirely pounded down.

It was a slow descent to the bottom. Rose felt like prey a predator had found in the forest and was dragging it back to feed the whole family. A feast for the thing in the freezer. That was where she was headed, and she needed an escape plan.

"Momma, why are you doing this?" Rose was on the edge of tears but swallowed them, thinking of Charlie from *Firestarter*. Rose wished she could will the entire basement to burst into flames. She would escape, take Sally with her, and they could live on together forever. But she was strong in her own way. She was mentally strong.

Rose used her free leg to begin the assault on the thing's oblique. It affected the thing; slowed it down. It appeared to affect Momma too. She and the creature were one and the same.

The path to the freezer wasn't being altered, so Rose took a gamble and rose, hopping on her free leg. She leapt opposite the stairs and grabbed hold of a pipe protruding from the hot water heater. The pipe held taut as the mindless thing tugged and tugged at Rose's leg. When it adjusted, it let loose a tad, and Rose took advantage. She pulled her leg free and used it to kick the thing's extended chin like the soccer ball she kicked around the yard with Sally.

The thing fell to the floor, and Rose was free. With a glance back, she watched the monster shrivel and use its clicking claws to clamber back into its safehouse.

When she was halfway up the stairs, she felt the sudden urge to peek inside the freezer when her view was capable. The smell wafted even from a distance, and that was what grabbed her attention first. A gaudy, mothball smell, typical of a basement.

Inside, wrapped in a fetal position was a gray alien-looking creature. It was short, and all 206 bones were visible through its transparent skin. It was executing sharp, jagged breaths as it performed hyper sleep. It looked peaceful in its slumber. A baby after a long day of crying and excitement. But it had turned Momma into a similar position. Momma was on the floor beside the chest freezer, curled in a ball with her knees drawn to her chest.

Rose was back upstairs, and Sally stood in the hall as she shut the basement door, throwing the lock in its place.

Sally wandered out of her bedroom, rubbing the sleep bits from her eyes as Rose was halfway down the hall.

"Are you crazy? Momma will kill you if she found you down there. C'mon, let's get you back to sleep," Sally said, taking Rose's hand and leading her back to her bedroom.

Rose felt odd not telling her sister about what she found downstairs. About Momma. About the creature that attacked her. But she wanted Sally safe. Was Sally strong enough to take on the basement monster?

Sally tucked her in and was exiting when Rose stopped her. "Sally?"

Sally groaned. She was tired, Rose could tell, and said, "What?"

"Do you think Momma is okay?"

"What do mean by that?"

"I mean she seems sad all the time now."

Sally pondered and said, "Yeah, maybe. I think her job is bad. That's probably why. Good night."

"Sally," Rose said in a whining tone.

"Yes, Rose."

"You would save me if something bad happened to me, right?"

Sally's face went pallor, and she corrected her slouching posture. "Of course," Sally said in a throaty way.

"Good."

"Why do you ask?"

"No reason. Good night, Sally."

Her sister shut off her lights and closed the door. Rose slept better knowing that whatever tomorrow brought, Sally would have her back.

Her big sister would be her savior.

CHAPTER 11

"How did you find me?" Momma said. It was impossible to see, even when Sally held out her hand in front of her face and moved it.

"Sheriff Winter passed along your address," Sally said, standing in the darkness of the bungalow. She was willing her eyeballs to adjust to the nothing around her, but Momma lingered, a blob of sporadic movement. Somebody or something could be lurking nearby, ready to attack, and Sally wouldn't be able to defend herself.

"Doesn't that man know when to keep his trap shut?"

Sally remained silent. This wasn't where she pictured her mother living. She envisioned her back in the home where it all started. It was a charred pile of wood, but Momma had moved out of there years ago.

"What did you want anyway?" Momma's voice was deeper than it used to be. It was possible she had picked up a cigarette habit since the day Sally left home.

"Oh, I found something." Sally had felt the weight of the envelope grow in her hand the longer she stood there.

The lie caused her stomach to churn. She had never lied to her momma growing up unless it was to protect Rose. But thirteen years later, revealing a white lie had turned her confused mental state into one of complete chaos.

A hand reached out. Sally watched as her sight adjusted to the long mucky fingernails and scabbed palms aching for a gift from the daughter of the owner.

Sally pressed the envelope to her chest, denying the hand.

"You need to tell me something first," Sally said.

A groan that might be released from the belly of a great fictitious monster filled the small room.

"Tell me what was inside the freezer in the basement."

That groan again. Her momma sounded in pain and delight at the same moment.

"You kids were never supposed to find that," Momma said. "I tried so hard to keep that a secret. I knew R—your sister was galivantin' down there, but I never thought it would come to that."

Sally winced at the pain it caused Momma to say Rose's name. Her own daughter. Her own missing daughter and she couldn't say her simple name.

"What happened?" Sally didn't want to know, but she needed to know. The secrets had gone on long enough.

"Do you even keep up with the local news?"

***

Sally felt like she should sit down. She felt Momma's story was going to be a long haul. But she wasn't offered a seat or able to maneuver herself to any type of chair without her vision.

"Now you're ignorin' me?" Momma asked.

The inquiry came out of the blue, and she assumed it was one of Momma's outlandish rhetorical questions.

"I don't keep up too much with the news, no." Sally had the lowest standard edition cell phone she obtained for free at the store. She could spend all day on the internet, surfing through social media, but she would rather escape real life into a book or writing of her own. She was shocked her momma, a supposed recluse, dabbled in the news channels.

Did she even have a television or cell phone? The calls she made to Sally were through a landline.

"Well, you should. One story in particular, at least. It happened in your neck of the woods a month or so back. A creature at a rest area. Ring any bells?"

Sally pondered at any oddity jangling around in her head, and she had a vague memory of two old men discussing something at the local coffee shop before heading to Redhill.

Sally slowly shook her head, unaware if Momma could see her.

"Well, that was your sister's doin'," Momma said.

Sally's eyes went wide, and a burst of unfiltered excitement flooded through her. Rose was still alive. She knew it. She could feel it. She couldn't keep the smile from forming on her tired face.

Reading Momma's expressions was impossible. The silhouette of her was oddly shaped. An oval head, but the outline was layered in a thick coating. Like frosting piped on the edges of a cake.

Momma was silent for a few seconds, and every second of quiet made Sally more uneasy. "What do you mean by that? How did Rose—"

"Never say that name in my dwellin', little girl." A momma of the past came through. The momma that would scold Rose for marking up the floor with a dash of washable marker. The momma that nearly killed Sally when she had her best friend, Ashlee, on the front porch talking. She had smacked Sally upside the head. Sally remembered waking up hours later with a bag of frozen peas on her temple, lying in the comfort of her own bed.

"Sorry," Sally said, her voice faltering.

"That little girl was always such a troublemaker. I gave her one rule. One. And she couldn't even do that. Daddy in the freezer was the last thing I wanted, but it was the only way."

"Daddy?"

"Shut your trap and listen. You never could learn to listen. Always interruptin' everybody."

Sally raised her hands, using the envelope as a reminder of what Momma's end goal was.

"It wasn't *your* daddy. It was the other one's. That was when the real problems started. Your daddy was the kindest, gentlest human bein' on this planet. I woulda been with him forever and beyond. But he just went on and died. Sleepin' right next to me. That was the saddest day of my whole life. It still gets me snifflin'."

Sally had heard little about her father other than he died when she was two months old. Rose's dad was a different story. Sally remembered his face and his problems. Drugs were a constant countertop blemish. A white powder on the side table. A little baggie of glass on the kitchen counter next to her bowl of Captain Crunch. Sally was at an age where those things meant nothing to her. They were just adult things she shouldn't be concerned with. If she knew now what she knew then, things would have gone differently. But one day he was gone. Momma had said he ran away with another mom. Sally was glad, but Momma seemed so upset by the news that Sally thought she had gone off her rocker. That was when the hitting and shouting started and never stopped. And that was when they weren't allowed in the basement anymore.

"Anyway. Enough with the sad talk. The other's daddy was a real rat bastard."

Sally was boiling, not from the weather but a heat that Momma must've kept at eighty degrees. The temperature on the outside was a cold that had receded a bit in recent days. A drop of rain hadn't touched the grounds of Redhill West in the past thirteen years, and the summers were brutal. The way Momma was still referring to Rose as an afterthought. As less than human. The heat she remembered from those sweltering months was nothing compared to what roiled inside Sally.

"A bad man. But he wasn't all that time. No, no, little girl. When we was first together, he was holding doors open and treatin' me to movies. Then came the drugs. There was some man named somethin'. He was supplyin' the stuff. One sniff and he was a different person. He was hittin' me and puttin' it inside me when I didn't want it there."

Sally did the most childish pose by placing her fingers over her ear holes and squeezing her eyes shut. All that was missing was the incessant, *La, la, la, I can't hear you. I can't see you. La, la, la.*

"Yeah, it's unpleasant hearin'. Imagine livin' through that."

She wanted nothing even remotely close to that image swimming around her imagination box. What she wanted was to get out of the small home as quickly as she could. She couldn't do that either. She felt Rose was somewhere close and she would find her.

"Livin' with an asshole like that came with lots of pain and misery," Momma said. It was the first time sadness had overcome her vocal range. It was like Momma was reliving those days from years ago over and over in her head.

"But he's gone now," Sally said. She wasn't contributing to the conversation, per se; she was creating a distraction to make a move.

Momma guffawed a crack of laughter. "That's what you think. When somebody's beatin' on ya, all you can think of is the good things. I didn't have no strength, no way. I was like a little kid against a bear. I felt each strike. One to the head, one to the stomach, one to the hip. I just had to sit there and take it. If I hit him back, he woulda just hit harder."

"But you were with him for so long," Sally said, taking two soft steps backward. She kept her hands behind her back to guide her away from anything she would potentially bump into.

"If you think five years is a long time, then you ain't never lived, little girl. Besides, what you know about relationships?"

One boyfriend she forced away with her past and one girlfriend she wished back into her life daily were her two loves in the twenty-two years of her lifetime. The relationship with the cute girl lasted three months. Sally loved her, but Sally was a broken person, and it put a ton of weight on the shoulders of the poor girl to do the necessary repairs. Sally cried herself to sleep for a week straight. And was still reeling from the heartbreak. Love was the greatest feeling in the world. The top of the food chain in euphoric human emotions. Feeling so many feelings for another person that they never left your mind was indescribable. Too was the feeling of that world crumbling around you. A heartbreak was viewed as a metaphoric feeling, but the chest pains each of those awful nights were very real.

"We had a life together," Momma continued. "Jobs to do. A home together. Our relationship went far beyond a point we ain't imagined. I woulda had to leave my only home. I woulda had to leave the town I love so much. I woulda had to—"

"Leave your two children."

The silence that followed the interruption felt like the winter's chill blowing across the tense air of the room. Sally shivered from the imaginary breeze. She was sure Momma would go on a rampage. That was the moment she would rise and strike down her oldest daughter.

"If I had left him, I woulda ended my life then and there."

That chill remained, but instead of a cold spine-chill, it was a soft autumn wind readying for a rough winter ahead. A sadness.

"Anyway, one day he comes home for the hundredth time gonked outta his gizzard. All different this time. Unrecognizable. I was so fed up with his childish ways that my blood was constantly boiling over like on a stovetop. I was so angry with him. He had the same process every day. Go to his job, go draw up some track marks, come home, sleep, eat, get a couple whacks on me, sleep, repeat. I was so glad he never bothered you."

She blocked out those years with Rose's daddy. The drugs and his face she remembered. His brown goatee wrapped his top lip and chin. His premature balding hairline halfway up his dome. His hazel eyes squinting each time she was in the same room. Sally assumed he never hit her because she stayed in her room while he was present.

"Some nights was worse than others. That one night was the worst. I ain't have to do nothin' that night to earn a beatin'. He was swingin' two steps into the door. You was sleepin'. It was like—like he was no longer a human. I had never seen him that bad before. He looked different too. Different how? I don't recall. Just bad. Could barely walk on his own two damn feet."

Momma refused to acknowledge the presence of Rose, who was in first grade at the time. Sally would see her in the school halls, and Rose would wave to her each time. A childish sporadic greeting. One Sally never gave in return because she was too damn smug to show her little sister any emotion in front of her friends.

"I tried my hardest to get outta the way. I never ran before, but that time it caught me off my guard. I just ran. I was outta that raggedy couch faster than you can say 'domestic violence.' In the kitchen I went for the knife, the big one in the draw. He shoved me so hard I smacked my chin on the counter. That one hurt like a bitch. After that I crawled to the next available door. The basement. I reached up and opened it. Now, I didn't do nothin'. I swear it. He was a druggy, and he tripped over the body he pushed to the ground. It was his own doin'. He went tumblin' down the stairs. I watched his face smack every other step. After, I spit out three of my teeth. Member I told you I brushed too hard?"

She didn't remember and didn't want to. Her search for some substance in Momma's home had turned up successful. A wall. A wall always led to somewhere. Was Momma so deep in her past that Sally would be able to slide along its base and find…anything?

"I stomped down the basement steps thinkin' he was gone for good. But at the bottom I saw his chest movin'. I swear I didn't think he would make it. He looked like he gone a hundred rounds with Muhammad Ali. My three teeth was nothing to his tic tacs scattered across the floor. His nose was a broken squiggle line. I swear his eyeball was poppin' out. He wasn't walkin' no more with the legs he had. He was gone for good. A wheezin' is what I heard from his mouth. Like a child's rattle toy. What was I to do?"

One step to the left and Momma was well on her way to a full-length novel at that point.

"I saw the freezer and I knew what I had to do. I couldn't call no police. Womens is always blame for their man's death. And there was no way I coulda proven I ain't do it. So, I took out all the frozen stuff. Chicken nuggets, TV dinners, ice cream, and threw it in the trash. Then I lifted his big ass and dumped him inside and closed the lid. I ain't want you goin' in there so I wrapped a chain around the outside. After I locked it, I thought it was over. But that was very far from the end of the story."

CHAPTER 12

Rose woke for the second time that week to Daddy on her bedroom floor. She thought he or Momma had caught her sneaking into the basement for her reading time in the early morning hours, but Daddy was always knocked out. Mondays were his days for Rose's bedroom floor. He slumbered in his own bed the rest of the days. One of those Mondays, Rose had poked him with her fingers, shoved him with her foot, and even climbed on top of him. He wouldn't ever wake up until the sun shone through the window. Then he would stand up, grab his belongings, and head out the door. Rose still snuck past his sleeping body to the basement, and his snores could be heard through the floorboards. She knew she wasn't caught…that time.

Now, he was snoring away early on a Thursday morning. Rose wasn't in a reading mood or a sleeping mood. She wished she could fall back asleep, but a loud daddy and a moving brain were not a good slumber combination.

Rose lifted the covers off herself and went into the kitchen. Momma said a warm glass of milk was a remedy for restlessness. Rose opened the cabinet and retrieved a drinking glass with a film of brown residue around the rim. All the glasses had obtained that over the years.

The main heating source, the microwave, was too loud for three in the morning, so she settled on cold milk. It felt great sliding down into her stomach. A refreshing drink that went best with cookies. Especially when she would help Momma with the chocolate chip variety.

As she set her glass in the sink, a door opened. She wasn't afraid. Momma, Sally, and Daddy were all in the house. It was her room opening, and Daddy stepped out. His eyes looked closed as he drifted down the hall, walking like a penguin to his next destination. He was coming toward her, but she wasn't sure he even noticed her until he spoke.

"Rose, what are you doin' outta bed, darlin'? It's late. Er, early. Whatever."

Rose stared up at him hovering over her. He was swinging back and forth like a buoy in the rough ocean. "G-getting a drink of m-milk," she said, her tone timid.

"There's plenty of time for milk tomorrow. You need sleep, baby girl. Now get back to your bed before I get your momma on ya."

"O-okay," she said and walked around him to her bed. She wished she had a lock on her door, but Momma wasn't one for privacy.

Under her tank tops, T-shirts, and other year-round inappropriate-for-the-season clothing, she pulled out a book. A book of her own creation. She fell in love with drawing since Sally had taught her a few things. She started with houses, then graduated to persons, and now she was creating her own world. Just like the books she read, she wanted her own made-up world.

In the world she was creating, she was the good girl. And surrounding her were the bad people. It wasn't a superhero story but a story where the good came out on top. Rose knew that mostly happened in make-believe. Real life never featured a good person winning in the end. Maybe if a bad person read the story, they could change their ways in real life.

She threw the covers over herself and clicked on the flashlight she kept under her bed. A pack of crayons and clipboard for a hard coloring surface was all she needed.

When she drew and fell into the story she created, it was like a kind of hypnosis. She felt she was present inside the drawings and living the lives of her characters. She drew what she knew. A nasty monster was ravaging the lives of the two girls escaping from the encampment they lived inside.

A pastel red triangle was Rose, and a bright yellow was Sally. They were holding hands, running away from the home, and behind them was a green ghoul. Sharp teeth filled its mouth, and a brown filth covered its disgusting, dripping face. It was much bigger and stronger than the two of them, but Rose knew Sally would protect her, and together they were unstoppable. They were running in the story, but they wouldn't run for much longer.

A toilet flushing brought her back to her covers shushing against her head. Daddy's footsteps left the bathroom, stomped creakily through the kitchen, and the door to her bedroom opened. She closed her book, plopped down, and hugged it to her chest. Her crayons had spilled and rolled against her legs. She clicked the flashlight off but wasn't sure if it was in time for him to see.

"Rosey, I'm sorry if I was rude back there in the kitchen. I didn't know what I was sayin'. Here, I brought you a fresh glass of milk." Each of Daddy's footsteps caused a ripple in her stomach as they grew louder.

The thin sheets were pulled over her head, but Daddy's breath could still be felt as he hovered over her and whispered.

"Rosey. Rosey baby."

Rose squeezed her eyes tighter as tears leaked from the corners. The sheet was being slid off, revealing her to the cold of the bedroom.

"I know you ain't sleepin'. Open them eyes and drink up."

Rose raised her eyelids, and he was closer than she thought. His face was haggard and tired. The lines across his forehead passed over one another like connecting rivers. His tattoo of a cobra swam on his left arm. He would tell Rose stories about how he caught one with his bare hands while he was fighting overseas and crushed its windpipe. She was scared of that story but fascinated with his bravery. His green eyes scanned Rose's exposed body before shoving the glass in her direction.

There wasn't much milk to speak of, and it looked spoiled to her. At least he warmed it up just the way she liked it. He watched on in anticipation as though she were the main star of a concert.

"I'm not thirsty anymore, Daddy," she said, handing the glass back.

He made no effort to grab it. "Is that so?" he said.

Daddy rose from his crouched position and left her room. Rose thought the worst was over. She had successfully chased Daddy from her room. He was impossible to force out on the other days he napped in there.

She sniffed the contents of the glass, and the milk he used must've been spoiled because she gagged at the scent. She placed the glass on her bedside drawer next to her favorite book, *Bridge to Terabithia*, which never left her bedside.

Daddy returned minutes later with his hands behind his back. He would surprise her with gifts when he came home from work sometimes. A nightlight for reading in the dark, a necklace she didn't want because jewelry made her skin itchy, and an electronic tablet he said she could read on but sat in her top dresser drawer untouched were some of the gifts he showered her with. Momma looked on each time with a distinct pain in her eyes. Rose never liked that look. She thought Momma was jealous because Rose got all the gifts and Momma received none.

"Got something for ya," he said and revealed a box with a bow on top.

"It's not my birthday," Rose said.

"It ain't gotta be ya birthday to get a gift, silly Rosey."

Rose snatched the box from his hands and lifted the top off. Inside was a first edition of Stephen King's *Firestarter*.

"I knew you was readin' it in secret, so I figured I just gift it to ya," Daddy said and sat on the edge of her bed.

Rose was beaming with joy. She had made it halfway through and was excited to see it through to the end.

"Oh, I love it," Rose said, hugging the hardback.

"I knew you would," he said and slid closer to her. "Now, I know your momma teached you manners, is that right?"

Rose nodded.

"Right, so if some person gives you a gift, you make sure to give somethin' in return. Does that sound right?"

Rose nodded.

"Okay. I gave you a book, now you gotta drink your milk for me. It makes ya bones nice and strong."

As he inched closer again, Rose scooched back. She was never terrified of Daddy, but she didn't like the days he slept in her room. Those once-a-week days were not fun for her. She squeezed tight on her eyes and her stuffed elephant. Her comfort buddy when Sally wasn't around.

"What's the matter? It's just yer daddy."

The cologne wafting from his skin was violating her nostrils. His hand grazed the outside of her arm and she nearly instinctively grabbed for her drawing book. *Firestarter* crashed to the floor. A thump that would surely wake Sally and Mommy.

When she held her drawing book tight in her arms, Daddy tried grabbing it from her.

"You don't need that right now, Rosey." She read the agitation in his voice.

His power over her was purely strength, but that won the battle each time. He lost his grip on the staple bounded stack of papers, and it flew through the air, landing in the center of the room. It opened to around the middle. Just before the part she was working on. It was a picture of her and Sally marching through tall trees encased by a black night sky. Sally was dragging her along to go to her secret hideout. A scene that came to her in a vision.

The last thing Rose remembered was Daddy rising from the bed. Then everything around them was made of paper. Daddy wasn't Daddy anymore. He was the gray monster she depicted in the book. Sally wasn't there next to her. Rose needed to fight him on her own.

CHAPTER 13

Sally removed her hand from the door handle she found in the dark. It was like she was in her old house all over again. A room she was sure she was forbidden to enter, and her momma close behind to scold her for such acts. But she was more interested in what Momma was saying.

"What do you mean by that?" Sally asked.

"I left Daddy in that freezer for a whole month before I even checked on him. I wanted to put him in the past. Leave him in there for good. But that bratty sister of yours never listened to a goddamn word I ever said. She just had to wander down there and be a kindergarten detective. I knew she was goin' down in that basement when she left the lock unlocked one day. It wasn't you cause you listen to me when I speak."

Sally leaned on the wall but affixed herself upright when the walls vibrated beneath her. It was like they were a living, breathing entity. Almost like they were affected by a strong gust of wind.

Momma continued. "I went down there one night. This was a week before that girl's final night."

Sally scoffed under her breath at the way Momma spoke about Rose.

"I was curious. Curiosity killed the cat and all that. I removed the chains from the freezer and opened it. What I found inside wasn't like nothin' I ever seen before. His body was stiff. He musta woken and tried pushin' his way out of the freezer. He was stuck in a position like a dog on its back. Paws in the air. He looked sad. I had a second where I felt bad for doin' what I did. Like I shoulda brung him to the hospital. He mighta survived. But he was a druggy. That was what he cared about the most. He was the walkin' dead every day. I didn't wanna look at him no more and chained it back up. Then, I saw the lock on the basement door undone. The girl had gone down. The next night, more like early fuckin' mornin', I followed her down. She was just readin' some old book my momma would read. I watched from the outside window. She was so innocent, sitting there readin' a grown-up novel. But just like my papa said, all punishments are necessary. I didn't want no normal 'go to your room' scoldin'. I wanted to teach her to never go into the basement again."

Momma released a guttural cough that sounded like it was coupled with a swab of phlegm and continued. "I had found something you're not gonna believe. Dead Daddy was givin' me some supernatural power. Like when I touched him, I would become him. And I ain't have control neither. It was like watchin' a movie. But it made me feel good. The first time I found that out, he tried to leave from the freezer and nearly busted out the basement. I had to snap out of it by bustin' him upside the head like he used to do to me. Then he crawled back inside and went back to his slumber. The second time was a scare. The third, well, I suppose you know the third time already."

Was the basement of this bungalow behind the door beside Sally? Was Rose down there right now? Sally needed to find out.

"I regret what I did. You gotta believe me," Momma said. But Sally was done listening to her woes about a past she could no longer control.

She turned the handle and the door opened.

"Please. Don't."

She wasn't sure what Momma didn't want her to do. Open the door? Go inside? Let the burning light in?

"Momma. I came here for one reason and one reason only. To find my little sister. If she is behind this door, I need to know."

A racked sigh came from Momma's direction. "I don't wanna punish you like I punished her. She deserved what she got. You don't. Don't make me do that. Just go back home."

Momma's voice was like she never heard it. Sally felt sympathy. For her momma. Sally knew she always did her best with what she had.

Sally opened the door wider. Lights from below guided her way to the descending steps.

"Before you go in there. There's one more thing you gotta know. I swear it, little girl. One more. Or you won't know what to make of it. You need to know about the drawings. About her drawings."

This stopped Sally in her tracks, even though she didn't want to hear another word from Momma.

The light held in by the wood door exploded into the small studio apartment-replica space. Sally snapped her hand over her mouth when she laid eyes upon Momma.

The skin on her face was melting like cheese off a hot pizza. Her nose was where her left eye should be, and her right eye was where her mouth should be. Her ear was her mouth and when her tongue exited to wet her sullen lips, drool dripped onto her shoulder. From the neck down, her naked body was exposed, and small cylinders filled her torso. It looked as though her pores had opened to the size of golf balls. Dark holes with no sight of what lay beneath them. Her feet were missing, and a wheelchair was her mobility. The bottom of each femur stuck out, making it impossible for her to walk ever again.

"I done told you," Momma said. Sally gagged, watching her ear-mouth form the words. "I done told you I gotta tell you what's goin' on. If you got down there, your eyeballs would roll out your skull."

It didn't matter what lay beyond her new and unimproved version of Momma. What could be worse than what she viewed now?

Momma flipped the brakes free of the horse and buggy wheels with her callused, burned hands. Momma rolled toward Sally, and Sally retreated down the first step.

"I can't stop ya from goin' down; I know that, little girl. Just know to expect the unexpected," Momma said.

Sally inhaled sharply and exhaled in slow patterns. It slowed her pumping heart rate and calmed her trembling extremities.

Expect the unexpected.

When Sally dropped into one of Rose's drawings, she wasn't expecting that. When she saw Momma, she wasn't expecting that. Her life had become the epitome of expect the unexpected.

But she knew deep down that what lay at the bottom of those steps was truly going to be unexpected.

CHAPTER 14

The proceedings of that fateful day, the day she was swept up and taken by a monster, still ran through Rose's head each morning she woke up in her momma's bungalow. It was as if the events occurred the day before. Crystal clear memories of being sucked into her own drawing in her own bedroom with her daddy. Rose was her own paper-thin self, but Daddy had become the tall gray monster she had created from the thoughts inside her head. She wasn't positive if that monster depicted Daddy, but all she knew was she needed to get away fast or stand and fight.

Rose was in awe and shock, but she had no time to feel feelings. A creature towering over her with a gurgling mass protruding from its mouth and skin drooling from its liquid body was hovering. Splats of the gray liquid were raining down on her. Each dot of liquid poked a hole through her paper skin.

She ran. Out of the copse of trees and into the grassy fields. It was like a stop action movie coming to reality. The blades were swaying in a stuttering motion. Like a video that hadn't fully buffered. Her movements were like snapshots moving her through life. That was all life was. Photos of memories that floated through your mind like pages of an album. What Rose knew well, even at the young age of six, was that everybody's photo album had a back cover sporting an obituary. She thought that day running for her life was her final page turn.

When she was inside the house, she had replicated their childhood home well enough with features such as the refrigerator with various blobs as magnets, as well as her

bedroom with a poorly drawn elephant signifying her pal
Squirt.

What she hadn't drawn was a paper book of the drawings
she currently ran through. The walls were crumbling like a
gingerbread house Sally and she had built one year around
Christmastime. The creature was burning the pages she
worked so hard to achieve with its slime. She stepped onto
the book that lay in the same spot at her real-life home, and
she was transported back into reality.

Her room was quiet, and the sun had begun to beam the
floor. For a moment Rose thought the light was a spotlight
on her drawing creation, but it had to have been a
coincidence.

Daddy was nowhere to be found. Not in her room, not in
the kitchen, not in the living room, not even when she
peeked into the basement from the outside window as Sally
and she waited for the school bus. He would have been at
work just as Momma had, but Rose had a feeling he was
never coming home again.

The very next day, Momma had thrown a lock on the
basement door and was adamant neither she nor Sally
venture down there. They had shared the same quizzical
look. Momma was a stickler for certain things. Cleaning up
a spill after you made it. Or doing your homework because
when Momma was a girl, she never did her schoolwork and
had to suffer through the heat of summer school. Those were
normal parent rules for the children. But keeping them out of
a certain room out of the blue seemed far from a simple
parental guidance.

"Ready for school?" Sally had busted into her room without knocking as she often did. Then Sally looked quizzical. "You okay?"

The Daddy incident was a month before, but the fight with the monster in the basement was the night before. Rose woke up sore and exhausted. She had tried to get back down there in the early morning hours, but she had misplaced the key. Momma was going to kill her for that.

Rose nodded and climbed to her feet. The dead-daddy monster had latched onto her ankle, and she was trying to not limp as not to alert Sally to any issues. She wasn't in pain so much as fear Sally would get mixed up in the past couple hours' endeavors.

School was a normal day. Math. Science. Music. Art. Coloring pictures the teacher provided. Rose must've looked like a nutcase placing the picture on the ground and trying to step into it. The colored book she kept in her bookbag was a special book. The only special book.

Normal snacks, normal lunch, normal bus ride home until Sally pulled her aside and said they were going on a little walk. Rose wanted to get back to her grown-up novel in the basement and her coloring, but she refused to be at home all alone.

It had been the final day of the school year, and Rose figured Sally wanted to surprise her with a present for making it through another year.

They trekked to the back yard and into the tall grass that grew past Rose's head. When they reached a train track, Rose didn't want to go any farther. She used the tracks as an excuse to avoid the woods. What she saw between the trees struck fear in her tummy. She watched as the gray daddy monster stalked her in the forest. Sally was looking away from the trees. She hadn't known if Sally could see the creature anyhow.

Sally had to be a grown-up quickly when Rose arrived. Daddy was never any help, and Momma did the best she could. Sally was playing the big sister and mother roles. It took Sally away from time with friends, plans she had to cancel, and Rose felt she was to blame. It got to Rose, the guilt of being a burden to others. It wasn't her fault she entered the world, and yet Sally was the best sister she could have asked for.

Rose hadn't planned on breaking her arm. She had planned on falling to create something dramatic. She was trying all she could to get Sally away from the creature prowling behind the firs and oaks. Rose hadn't expected Sally to go on without her. Her plan had fallen apart in seconds, and the creature scooped her up. Sally froze with fear instead of helping her. Rose never forgave her for that. Sally was strong. Sally could have fought the thing off. Sally had made a promise to protect her, but she failed to follow through.

Now, being in the basement of Momma's bungalow and fearing absolutely nothing was how she wanted to live out her life. Rose's first creation, the book of drawings, was the only item she removed from their childhood home before she torched it to the ground. It had all gone according to plan until Sally had escaped the drawing. The plan was to get to get Sally inside, then burn the book. Ridding her of a sister forever.

Rose's scribblings were magic. She could trap people inside never to be released, which she had accomplished many times. And her drawings could be brought out of the page and into the real world. It was a power she never wanted to let go of again. She wielded her pencil like a maniac with a sword. Trapping bad guys inside and releasing monsters to the outside.

When she saw Daddy on the news, recorded on somebody's phone, the gray creature terrorizing the citizens at a Connecticut rest area, something had changed in Rose. When she saw him at the claw machine trying to win a stuffed elephant, she knew it was her daddy. She knew he would bring her one true love back. Her Squirt.

When her drawings came to life for the first time, Rose was afraid. Then a pleasure had taken her over. She didn't have control over the minds of what she created and released. So, the teen creature who killed his girlfriend, the mall creature who went and killed itself outside of a PacSun, and the ballpark creature who streaked across the baseball diamond and was tackled and killed by security were all disastrous. First, it was a way to find Daddy. A connection to him. If he was a drawing she created, maybe her other drawings could find him. After so many years of nothing, she became unhinged.

The drawings were believed to be parts of normal society. Flesh and bone from the mind of a growing girl in a basement. It was a dangerous tool she was playing with. Like releasing a swarm of bees into a small classroom. Some would be stung; others would get away unscathed.

But the successes made her ecstatic. The creature that shot a crooked cop dead in the streets. The creature that collapsed a factory producing mass amounts of methamphetamine. And Rose's number one project, her momma. That was a job she worked hard at for many weeks. She needed to perfect the woman who singlehandedly ruined her life.

But that was all water under the bridge now. Momma sat upstairs bound to a wheelchair, and Rose had all the freedoms in the world. If she wanted a banana, she drew it and ate it. If she wanted books, she drew one, and it came to life. All she needed was at the tip of her pencil. She hadn't left the basement in thirteen years.

Momma was the one to keep her down there. When Momma found her in the forest three days after the taking, Momma scooped her up and brought her home. Sure, she fed Rose, bathed her, treated her broken arm, and gave her head a pillow to rest. But Momma cared more about herself than her own daughter. When Momma lost her job, she panicked as she often did. Any food that came in went ninety percent Momma, five percent Sally, and five percent Rose. Rose was her secret prisoner because she could never take on the task of two humans. So, she kept Rose in the basement just as she did Daddy.

What Momma failed to realize was that Rose was slowly torturing her mind. Her time in the basement with pencil and paper was mesmerizing. When Rose discovered her talent, space was the limit. When Daddy and Rose fell into her drawing, Rose escaped, and though Rose didn't witness the escape, she suspected Daddy came back a changed person. He became the monster in the coloring book.

What Momma needed to be was trapped with no way out. She needed to be punished for her dirty deeds.

Over the years in the cellar, Rose worked tirelessly at her craft. Perfecting her drawings to the realism of true life.

Each crevice of the home blended seamlessly together. Each crack the correct shape and length. Unrecognizable as her own home.

Years after Sally went to Connecticut to live with their aunt, Momma moved Rose, her prisoner, to the bungalow. Rose was excited. Momma had released her from her grasp, but Rose chose to plop herself in the basement. That move was the worst mistake of Momma's life. As she drew her trap, she listened to Momma whine on the phone about her new job and the people around her. After many failed attempts to pull Rose from the cellar, Momma turned into a servant. Dropping food at the same time throughout the day. Forgetting her younger daughter existed.

Seven years later, Momma had walked into the trap. Momma was inside Rose's artwork without recognizing a difference until she saw a flaw in the art. A simple mistake, and Momma went berserk. She tore at the paper walls, and the floor moved from beneath her, sending her back into her real-life bungalow. Momma was so angry she readied the police on the phone. Rose decided the best course of action was to cut Momma's feet right from underneath her.

During the scuffle, Rose tackled Momma, and her spine suffered the brunt of the impact. While she lay there for weeks, Rose drew up the perfect portrait for Momma to wear.

When she finished, Rose rolled Momma to the mirror to see the beauty Rose had turned her into.

Rose removed all sharp objects and rope from the house after Momma's three failed suicide attempts. Momma was going to feel the torture she put her own daughter through. She would feel Rose's pain until her heart gave its final beat.

Now, footsteps on the stairs didn't scare Rose. She knew who the visitor was waltzing down into her dungeon. Though she hadn't seen Sally in thirteen years, she somehow looked the same. A bit older with age lines at such a young age.

I can buff those out for you, sis, Rose thought.

"What happened to you, Rose?"

The voice was deeper and more mature.

"I'm having the time of my life, Sal."

CHAPTER 15

By the time Sally reached the bottom of the steps and
Momma was left alone in the darkness, Sally felt like she
entered a different world. She wasn't a poorly drawn paper
version of herself. She remained in her bone and skin, but all
around her was change.

The four walls holding them in were moving in waves. It
was as if the ocean was continuously crashing into the
support of the drywall. It made no sound but was visible to
the naked eye. Rose sat in the center of the square basement.
Stacks of paper were like skyscrapers touching floor to
ceiling. The stacks were pillars holding the small bungalow
in place. Peeks of the hardwood floor could be seen beneath
the countless drawings. These drawings were much more
complex than the last she had seen by Rose. The lines were
impeccable. The definition of the person's skin and features
was so realistic that Sally was cautious to step on them.
Although it may have been to avoid falling into another
artist's rendering rather than destroying her work. Sally
didn't know how that worked, but having experienced it one
time around was enough.

"I knew you'd come looking for me. You always said
you would save me, protect me," Rose said.

It was surreal to be peering down at a teenage girl lying
on her stomach with her ankles crossed, swinging her calves
loosely while she shaded a picture of the Taj Mahal. Rose's
blonde hair had faded to a darker red, its length not touching
her shoulders. The high cheek bones that were Rose's
standout feature had sunken to nothing.

"Rose. I don't—"

"You don't need to say anything."

"No. I don't understand. How is any of this possible?"

Rose lifted herself from the ground and sat cross-legged. "The short answer is I don't know. The long answer is I can tell you what I do know, and you can figure it out for yourself."

"Momma told—"

"Momma told you her side of the story. She was always so full of herself. Everything was always so awful for her. Everything was always my fault. If you want to know the true story. The story from the mouth of the kid who actually experienced all of the bullshit—"

Sally was a bit taken aback by the vulgarity. It was tough watching her little sister go from a young child enjoying simple tasks such as reading a children's book to hoarding her own artwork in the basement of her momma's bungalow. Their momma who wasn't the same. And Sally was beginning to realize Rose had much to do with that.

"—her mother had put her through."

Sally tiptoed to the opposite side of the room. She rounded her sister, not getting too close.

"I'm not gonna bite, Sal. But I can certainly draw something that can." Her laugh was wicked and uncomfortable to listen to. The cute softness she had once before dashed by years of hermit life.

"Okay, Rose. I want to hear. Tell me your tale of woe."

Rose shot a candid look at Sally, and then her face went slack. Sally knew she was in for the long haul. There was nowhere to sit in the basement, but the feeling of dread refusing to exit Sally's inners triggered her fight-or-flight response. Unsettled was a term she hadn't used often, but that was how she felt in the same room as her grown-up baby sister.

***

"Hm," Sally said when Rose had finished her sob story.

"What is that supposed to mean?" Rose asked.

"It doesn't mean anything. I just thought you treated Momma unfairly."

Rose stopped doodling. She was working on a beautiful rendition of the white house now. Her edges and shadows were unmatched. Sally had an urge to gush about how realistic and lifelike her artwork was, but it wasn't the time nor place. The place, now looking like cooked pasta being tossed around in a pot, was on its way to a crumbling stage. Sally wanted to run but held steady.

"Unfairly? She locked me in a cellar for most of my adult life. Are you fucking kidding me, Sal?"

"She was doing what was best for you."

"Best for—" Rose stopped and rubbed her cheeks that no longer held their red pallor. A single characteristic that would have held the baby-Rose she knew and loved. "You have lost your mind in the last thirteen years."

Sally turned and was inadvertently directing Rose's attention to the paper mess that had consumed her life for so long. "Me? Rose, you could have left this place long ago. Momma wasn't holding you hostage. She was keeping you safe. I was keeping you safe."

Rose stopped her shading and dropped her pencil on the west wing. "You watched as I was taken by a monster. Tell me, Sally. How were you keeping me safe?"

"I was taking you away from that house. The way you were keeping me safe from the monster in the woods. I was removing you from the situation with Momma and your dad."

A loogie landed as Sally's feet by way of her younger sister. "I don't need your safety. I can take care of myself fine. I'm doing just fine."

"You are sitting in a prison cell of your own mind. And worst of all, you placed yourself inside and threw away the key. Look around. And I mean really look around. Look beyond the paper, beyond your drawings. What do you see?"

A flash of the old Rose shone through. Her wonderful ocean eyes and cute little chin dimple were there for only a second, but it appeared. Then, she snapped back to present-day Rose. "I see the world outside. Through the television when Momma wants it on. Through the window at the front of the bungalow. And I ask myself, why would I want to live in such an awful place? I have all I need right in front of me. And if I need something in the outside world, I just draw it to life."

How had Rose become so delusional? She was living a life through the eyes of others. Our individual selves and accomplishments were what made us human. Sally traveled the United States because of the books she wrote from her brain. It was a creation of fiction, but her own experiences shone bright on each page. Rose's drawings were of no substance. She still had that kid's mind. Wanting things for the sake of wanting.

"How many do you have out there?" Sally asked.

"How many what?"

"People you drew that commit these—whatever they do."

Rose pondered. She tapped her perfectly manicured finger to her chin. "Somewhere between three and five thousand."

Sally had felt in control of the conversation. Had felt she was on the road to convincing her baby sister to step outside these shaky walls. But now she was rendered speechless.

"I lost count after the first thousand," Rose said absently.

"And what are they doing?"

"I don't know," Rose said with a childish shrug. "I can't control their actions. I can try. I try to control it, and it would work if it wasn't for stupid people. The human race is destroying the world. And if I replace them with my people, then—"

Sally took two steps toward Rose and smacked her across her left cheek. Rose recoiled her head and rubbed the reddening spot. Sally had no premeditation to her action; she thoughtlessly slapped her sister.

"The fuck was that for?"

"To get you to wake up. C'mon." Sally took the string bookbag off her back and opened it.

"What's in there?" Rose asked, rubbing her cheek.

"This."

Rose's face wasn't evil any longer. It was as if her stuffed elephant had been holding the key to release the devil from within herself.

"You—I—thought it was lost forever. It can't be the same one because—"

Sally twisted the animal around, and hanging from its butt was a string tail Momma had sewn on after Sally accidentally tore it off during a rough playtime. The white stitching held it together.

Tears rolled down her cheek and she reached for it. Sally snatched it back to her person and with her other hand still in the bag, she removed Rose's own book of drawings and flung it at her face.

She wasn't sure what the outcome would be, but she found out fast.

Rose stumbled backward and fell into the spaghetti wall. Like a papier-mache covering two wire beings created by an artist, the sticky, papery walls were suffocating Sally. She racked her arms to break or reach the end of the material. She feared there was no end. She screamed, but the material muffled her sound, and with each inhale gasp, the material fluttered in her gape. A gluey, expired water flavor reached her taste buds, and panic set in. She had a flash of being a ghost on Halloween night fifteen years ago.

Momma had taken the girls out one year for trick or treating. Rose wore pink and blue butterfly wings, and Sally draped a white sheet over herself with two circles cut out for eye holes. The three of them wandered down Carbridge, stopping at each house for a handful of the best candy. After wandering to the two streets that bookended Carbridge, they were back home with a table full of candy and an irrational momma.

"That's not fair, Momma," Sally had said.

"Life ain't fair, then ya die," Momma said, swiping both their sacks of candy from them and dumping all their hard work into the trash. "I won't have you kids eatin' this for breakfast, lunch, and supper. You're gonna rot your teeth. Trust me." Momma bared her yellowed and blackened smile at the leering and sobbing kids.

"We are not—"

"The discussion is over. Now go to your rooms; you got school tomorrow."

Sally felt stupid crying over something as meaningless as candy, but it was a fun activity with a great reward, and it was snatched away and gone within seconds. She didn't sleep for the first few hours that Halloween night.

At around two in the morning, her bedroom door creaked open. Sally snapped her eyes shut in case Momma was checking up on her.

"Here," a small voice squeaked.

Knowing it was Rose, Sally opened her eyes to see her, the costume wings still hanging askew on her shoulders and a pillowcase full of candy.

"Wh—wh—how did you get that?" Sally asked.

"From the trash. I got it for you."

Sally had stopped her crying hours ago, but she had an extra tear for her baby sister. She leaped out of bed and hugged Rose. They shared chocolates, jaw breakers, and apple slices from the one house that handed them out for the next hour and shared their most precious asset, time.

That was the early morning Sally told Rose all about her treehouse. What she kept inside. What she did in there. Even what it smelled like.

Now, Sally was reminded of that smell. Not chocolate or fruity tooth killers, but a pinewood stench that stuck inside her nostrils each time she reached the top of her favorite hangout.

The papery material was off and gone. Instead, she was surrounded by that sweet-smelling wood. Her thinking place. Her crying place. And she was just in time for the latter.

Sally often worried about Rose's future. It was something she thought every big sibling was concerned about their younger counterparts. Would they get into trouble with the law? Would they become addicted to drugs? Would they become a recluse who drew pictures and stayed in a basement for years? Fear pitted her stomach at every thought.

"How did I get here?" Sally asked the empty treehouse.

She scanned the outdated posters of boy bands she enjoyed. Wrappers from candy she wasn't supposed to have. It was her escape from everyone and everything. And being there now as an adult, the space too tight, the wood creaking under her heavier body, the fetal position she was forced into made her think of Rose. It was how Rose was inside her own mind. Trapped in a confined space. And she needed to get out.

Sally pushed herself to the rectangular opening, her hair hanging at each side of her face as she peered down and saw wood planks that were to be treated as rungs on a ladder. Some had fallen off and sat at the pit at the bottom of the oak. But that wouldn't impede her climb down.

Once at the bottom, she had wished for the vast areas of tall grass up to her waist, but all that grass had burned away, leaving an empty field of dead foliage, worn couches, dirty mattresses, squished cardboard boxes, and an array of filled black garbage bags. Her special place had been turned into a landfill. A tear struck her cheek, but the time for sadness ended when the ground shook, nearly knocking Sally to the filthy soil.

She turned and wrenched her neck to look forty feet above her. The night sky that hadn't produced rain in thirteen years was covered by a pale monstrosity that was once her mother fee fi fo fumming toward her. Hands lifted Sally from behind, and Rose said, "We need to go."

As they ran in the direction of what would have been their home, Sally recognized where she was. The bungalow Momma lived in was the work of her sister. It was an artist's rendering of a home come to life. And the monster Rose had created to torture Momma was going to take both of her daughters out of this world with one giant stomp.

CHAPTER 16

When the town of Redhill was being split into sections and the loners were fighting to keep the shitty west side of town the way it was, Sally remembered lying in bed at night, listening to the massive booms that would shake the home. She prepared for the roof to collapse upon herself and become buried alive under the rubble.

The actuality was the town rock blasting the large rock walls that ran along the line between Redhill East and Redhill West. The outdated walls that were blown away and replaced with homes, roads, and a mall. It kept the east residents and the west residents happy in their little bubbles. Whenever Momma would take them into the east for clothes or any food the convenience store failed to carry, Sally and Rose would discuss which house they would grow up in. They ended up living different lives, and the fact that they had come together was a miracle.

That rock blasting sound was approaching them from behind, and the sisters needed to work together to escape the approaching momma monster. The truth was Momma wasn't the monster in the home all those years ago. Up until Rose's father began living with them, Sally loved coming home to Momma and tolerated Rose as much as a big sister could. He was the monster. But Momma was to blame for keeping him around. She was the adult, and she needed the strength and courage to toss him out of their lives. Momma looked defeated each day.

The open field of garbage that was previously Sally's escape was taken over by Momma as she had seen her in the house. Her face a Picasso painting and her body a paper silhouette at a shooting range. Normal-sized Momma no longer lived. The bottom of her femur landed feet away from the running daughters. It was like a white boulder dropping in on them from the sky. Sally glanced up; Momma's tongue lolled out like a sleeping bag unrolling. The tip whisked her spotted shoulder.

"Toward home," Rose said, looking back to see if they gained any distance on the monstrosity after them.

"Why? It's a pile of nothing." Sally said each word between inhales and exhales. Sally was naturally skinny for most of her life. Pizza, donuts, and bagels were on her daily diet, but her metabolism kept her at a steady rail-thin weight. Rose was a cute chubby kid and had a few extra pounds on her now. But Rose was outrunning Sally by a long margin.

"Here, help me," Rose said.

Sally arrived a full minute later, not ready to exert any further energy. However, a ground-shaking slam of the thing's lack of foot reminded Sally that she hadn't a choice.

Pieces of scorched siding were the easiest to remove from the pile. Hunks of splintered 4x4 wood pieces were the toughest. Rose propped her legs against an exposed dresser that was cut in half and resting on a remaining part of wallboard. Sally pulled from the other side until the heavy wood was dislodged. This opened a gap. When Sally looked down, the top of the white chest freezer was showing through.

"You need to drop down," Rose said.

"Why? You need to explain what's happening," Sally said. Their heads snapped simultaneously at the thunderous boom.

"This is not a good time," Rose said.

"This is the perfect time because I don't know what I'm doing down there."

Rose huffed a breath out and said, "Okay. When I sent my daddy into the picture, something happened. I escaped back into the real world, and he didn't. I thought he was trapped in there, so I left my drawings on my nightstand for the next week. When I opened it, the monster I drew was gone. That was when the freezer was chained up by Momma. He must've escaped and attacked Momma in the night, and Momma fought back. When he was in the freezer, he got all weird. Momma let him out one night and he attacked me like I told you. What I didn't tell you was Momma was acting as weird as he was. She was just watching on as Daddy attacked me. Like she was hypnotized. The next day was when I was taken."

The ground shaking had stopped in Sally's mind, but the momma monster was growing ever closer. It stood a few steps away.

"That can't be possible." Though after experiencing falling into Sally's drawings and seeing what they could become, Sally knew it was a probability. Even as she peered around her, the momentary dizziness caused Sally to catch herself. Although, it was unclear if that was inside her head or the earth tilting on its axis.

"I fell into a trance after that," Rose continued. "I became power hungry with my drawings. I wanted Momma to suffer. I wanted you to suffer. I wanted the world to suffer. I planned on drawing a whole community of people to take over the other humans. Create my own human race. I needed a wake-up call, and you were it. I was so inside my own head; I couldn't see straight. And now I've got us into a mess I'm not sure I can get us out of. There is one more chance and it's inside that freezer."

The shimmer on Rose's cheeks de-aged her many years. Her sobs were so childlike. Sally had no response. She pulled her elbows in and, like a trained diver, dipped feet first inside the hole. The basement surprisingly had that same damp, desolate smell as she lay on top of the freezer and rolled off to the cement floor.

"Open the freezer up. Underneath the floor ice liner there is a drawing. Get it and bring it back here," Rose said.

The freezer lid opened enough for Sally's petite stature to slide inside and pull up the ruglike liner on the bottom. Folded in the crevice of the rectangular box was a piece of white paper folded in fourths. As Sally unwrapped the frozen paper, it revealed a gorgeous drawing, an early Rose drawing, of just that, a red rose. Sally pocketed it, and as another step came from above her, the rubble shifted. The hole shrank, leaving no room for Sally to escape.

"Shit. Sal. Are you okay?"

"Yeah, try moving some things." Sally was trying to keep her voice steady, but her fear had overtaken her body.

"I…ugh…can't."

Sally searched for something to open the hole back up. There was nothing. The top half of the stairs was crushed under the weight of the collapse. The boxes of books were unburned but unhelpful. The boiler and furnace were accordioned, and the cement stand holding them in place was settled for only those with inhuman power to move.

"What does this picture do?" Sally asked through the bowling-ball-sized hole. Rose's face filled the porthole.

"It takes us back. Well, it should."

"Back to where?"

"Back to the beginning. When we were walking away from Momma. We found a rose. It was a random one," Rose said with a chuckle. "In the middle of the grass. You remember?"

Sally nodded. It had entranced Rose. It had entranced both of them.

"It was the first thing I drew," Rose continued. "When Momma found me after Daddy dropped me. It was the first thing I remembered. When I was forced into the basement, I snuck it inside the freezer, but I tried it first. I stuck my head through, and you were standing next to me, just as you had been that day. You were so calm even with all that was going on in that home. I knew you were saving me. Pulling me out of that bad situation. I swear it, Sal. That must be what it does."

The bowling ball size shrank to softball size when Momma was one giant step away.

"Here," Sally said, reaching the paper through the hole.

"No, you need to come with me. Sally, I can't leave you behind, please. I'm sorry. I'm sorry for what I did to you."

"The momma-thing will be gone, and you will be safe. Start over again. Do it the right way. You will have a second chance. Take the paper, Rose. You are a good person. I know you can do good things. Help people."

The iced paper left Sally's hands. She couldn't see but could hear the paper crinkling in her sister's hands. Rose was going back to where she belonged. Rose was part of the living. Rose was going to make a difference in the world. Rose was—

CHAPTER 17

"Where are we going?" the young teen girl with a bob haircut said.

The young boy pulling her arm with loving care strutted past the movie theater tucked into a strip of storefronts with Harry's Hardware, Lulu's Nail Salon, and Mike's Vape Shop. The mouth of the alleyway that split the theater and Harry's was a chain-link fence that stopped the couple twenty feet from the road.

"Hm," the young boy with brown hair flopping at his neck said.

"We need to go over?" the young girl asked.

"Or—"

The young boy yanked a piece of the fence that looked to have been cut out by some hooligans a time ago. It was enough space for them to slip under and through to the other side.

There was a field of the greenest grass and the bluest sky. They ran. Not fast but enough for them to hold pace with one another.

"This isn't anything I could've imagined for a first date, but I love it. I really do," the young girl said.

"This is only the beginning, c'mon."

Another ten minutes and they came to a clearing. It was desolate and a bit scary to the young girl. It was the side of town her father warned her of going.

"What are we doing here?" The young girl's tone shifted from trust to fright in a matter of seconds.

"You'll see," the young boy said.

"No, I refuse to go until you tell me where we're going. I know this area as a bad one. Murders and robberies. It's going to get dark soon, and I'm not looking to get robbed."

"Do you trust me?"

That was a loaded question for the young girl. They had met at a coffee shop, rolled a game of bowling, then ventured into the streets on the journey that led them to this very spot. She made the decision to climb into his vehicle to ride between activities. That alone showed her trust in the young man. He showed no signs of hatred or anger within the five hours of time together. She had wanted to kiss him a couple times but refused to give in to her wants.

The young girl shrugged. It was all she could reply with.

"If you trust me," the young boy said, holding out his hand to her, "then take it. You won't regret it."

With regret, she folded her palm in his. It was warm and comforting.

When he shot off again, she kept up. Her perfect short curls she put so much effort into were blowing and surely unraveling in the wind as they rounded the corner of an old rundown, unoccupied bar. Along the side of the establishment was a cement wall with a mural. It was magnificent. Graffiti markings had littered the masterpiece, but it was easy to see.

One stick figured girl stood in front of a bundle of trees. She wore a triangle dress, and as the young girl studied the drawing, she could imagine the little girl in the drawing reaching out. Her hand was upstretched and looked to be aching, waiting for somebody she loved to grab it.

"This is—"

"Incredible. I told you."

The young girl stepped forward to feel its artistry. She wanted to know how it was accomplished. Her hand reached forward.

"Hang on a sec," the young boy said. "Before you go in there, you might want to take this."

Her date dug in the bookbag he carried and tossed her a rain poncho. The three lines that formed in the middle of young girl's forehead showed she had no idea what she was walking into.

"It's raining," the young boy said.

She peered up into the sky sinking into a pre-nighttime magenta. "I can see it's clearly—"

"Trust me. It's raining," the young boy said and pulled on his poncho as did she.

The young boy reached in hand first, his other clasped in his date's. He then entered with his body like crossing the threshold into the shower and was blasted by a downpouring waterfall of rain. The golden sun shower burst with its full intensity as they walked in together.

The young girl wasn't held down by any emotion. The vitamin C and calming pattering of rain was as welcoming as the first day of preschool.

"Where are we?" the young girl asked but wasn't concerned.

In the distance, through the hazy fog was an elephant, its trunk tilted upward, spraying a fireman's hose constant of water.

"We are on the other side. The other side of the universe."

"Can we go back?"

"Do you want to?"

A smile landed on the young girl's face, and her love smiled right back.

Why would anybody want to? the young girl thought. *Why would anybody want to?*

Edited by: Sara Kelly
Cover Design: Elderlemon Design

About the author

Joe Baldwin was born and raised in the idyllic state of
Connecticut where he received his degree in Criminal Justice.
When he is not nose-down in a book you can find him on a long
walk beside the roar of traffic or attempting to befriend his pug-
tailed tabby cat named Piranha. Joe is the author of THE GAME
AND OTHER STORIES.